Forbidden Legacy

2391

Barbara Masci Goss

SPIRE

© 1989 by Barbara Masci Goss

Published by Fleming H. Revell
a division of Baker Book House Company
P.O. Box 6287, Grand Rapids, MI 49516-6287

New Spire edition 1994

Printed in the United States of America

Library of Congress Cataloging-in-Publication Data

Masci Goss, Barbara.
  Forbidden legacy / Barbara Masci Goss.
       p.   cm.
    ISBN 0-8007-8621-1
    I. Title.
  PS3563.A7817F6 1989
  813'.54—dc20   89-32658

Scripture quotations in this volume are from the King James Version of the
Bible.

Forbidden Legacy

1

The stagecoach bumped over the deeply rutted trail. When it didn't bump, it lurched. As it swung wildly to the right, a fat, grubby hand fell on Sarah Clarke's knee. Discreetly, she edged her legs as far from the man on that side as space allowed, but in so doing succeeded—much to her chagrin—in raising the eyebrows of the small, distinguished young gentleman on her left. Immediately she swung her legs straight, relieved the knees she now brushed belonged to her great-aunt, seated opposite.

Aunt Emily affectionately patted Sarah's bruised and travel-worn limbs. "Are you comfortable now, my dear?" she asked solicitously.

Sarah smiled. "Yes, and thank you. But what about you? You're three times my age, and you haven't complained yet. Surely you are as bruised and sore as I."

Emily winked. "I'm seasoned."

"Seasoned?"

"Do you think I always lived the life of luxury with you and your mother, in Chicago? Remember, only the past five years have I lived like a queen with you two. It was wonderful to be invited, but I prefer to do for myself. Always did. I got my education deep in the hills of Pennsylvania."

"I know. Mother told me so many times how poor you and she were then. I'm glad you aren't living like that now." Sarah patted her aunt's knees.

"We would have been lucky to be *poor*; we were *destitute* before your mother was born. By good fortune, the next generation *was* poor. Our dad, like yours, was killed by Indians, but unlike you, we witnessed the whole thing and hid to save ourselves. After that, we didn't know where our next meal would come from."

"How terrible," Sarah sympathized.

"Well, Dad's death was, but the life was wonderful—wouldn't trade it for anything."

"You wouldn't?"

"No, it seasoned me. We worked, and we worked hard, but we learned plenty. Struggling drew our family closer." Aunt Emily sighed. "No, you can have your maids and nannies. I always say, 'If you want a job done right, you do it yourself.' "

"I'm glad you offered to come to Texas with me. Mother would never have let me come alone," Sarah said.

"My pleasure. I was glad to get away from that cold, rich mansion and those servants who even try to blow your nose for you!" Emily chuckled at Sarah's grimace as the other passengers, who pretended not to listen, tried hard not to smile.

An old man next to Emily Ruggles began telling her about his hard life, and the two began an animated conversation.

Leaning back, with eyes closed, Sarah tried to relax amid the coach's crushing jolts and sudden heaves. Breathing deeply to ease her tensions, she recognized the scent of leather and the mixed odors of horses and sweating human bodies. She marveled at her ability to smell at all, with so much dust in her nose.

The constant rocking and creaking of the carriage began to lull her tired body. She'd almost relaxed enough to fall asleep when a shrill cry from the top of the stagecoach jarred her to attention.

"Indians!"

Indians! Her eyes flew open and darted about fearfully. Not only had her father been killed by them, the ladies at the Topeka stop had related lurid tales of their savagery.

Sarah's heart fluttered as the six carriage occupants braced themselves. The stagecoach raced forward, despite the condition of the trail. The driver could be heard coaxing the horses into an even faster run.

"Aunt Emily, *Indians!*" Sarah cried, unable to keep still a moment longer.

"Don't worry, dear." Aunt Emily patted her great-niece's knee. "The driver and his friend will know what to do."

Wide-eyed, Sarah looked at the other passengers. The quiet, dignified gentleman on her left removed his spectacles and nervously wiped the dust from them with his handkerchief. Beside Aunt Emily sat a heavy-set teenage boy whose eyes attentively sought his grandfather, seated on Emily's other side. The old man choked the neck of his cane with wrinkled, white hands, until Sarah thought his protruding blue veins would burst.

On Sarah's right, the obese man with the wandering hand had decided to brave a peek out the window.

With his head back inside the coach he reported, "There's only a handful chasing us."

"How many does it t-take to be dangerous?" asked the boy, with wide eyes and flushed cheeks.

The man shrugged. "With four armed men, we should be able to handle 'em. They ain't even wearing war paint," he complained, as if he'd been cheated. "Ya do gotta gun, don't ya?" he asked the quiet man on Sarah's left.

Before the gentleman could answer, a loud crack rendered them all speechless. Crazily, the coach skidded, accompanied by a deafening scraping noise. Then Sarah realized the

screeching and sliding had stopped—but so had the coach—
and with Indians chasing them!

The driver and the express manager leaped down from the
driver's perch and examined the stage's underbody.

"Everybody out. We've broken an axle," shouted one.

"Don't worry, we have the Indians covered," hollered the
other, aiming his double-barreled shotgun toward the thun-
dering cloud of dust rapidly approaching them.

Praying her legs would accommodate her, Sarah climbed
down from the coach with the others.

Through the dust Sarah watched the Indians rein in their
small, scraggy horses. Standing near the coach, her heart
raced frantically. She awaited her doom.

The small, quiet gentleman who'd ridden beside her since
Topeka leaned toward her and whispered, "These Indians
don't appear to be attacking, miss. They have no guns or war
paint." Seeing her colorless face, he asked, "Are you all
right?"

Sarah found her voice weak, "Yes, thank you."

The obese man who'd also ridden beside Sarah joined the
two men with guns, crouched at the rear of the stage. This
reassured Sarah somewhat, for now a rifle, a shotgun, and a
six-shooter were all aimed at the eight ragged, dust-encrusted
Indians.

The dark, leather-faced men with long, stringy hair dismounted and approached the passengers. On the ground
they appeared shorter yet no less formidable, with high
cheekbones and long, thin, hollow faces.

The tallest, apparently the leader, approached Sarah.
Stretching out his hand, he swiped at her head. She shrank
back, unwilling to let the savage touch her.

The leader called laughingly to the others, "Corn-topped
lady fear for scalp! She 'fraid!"

While the Indians laughed, the gentleman beside her
whispered, "Let him touch your hair. That's all he wants.
Indians don't often see blond hair; he is amused by it."

Inwardly Sarah cringed as the redskin roughly caressed her hair. Deliberately putting on a brave face, she looked up at him defiantly, as if daring him to harm her.

With a taunting smile and squinting black eyes, he measured her before clumsily lunging for her throat. Sarah held her bold look, trusting he wouldn't discover her fear by the rapid throbbing of her neck pulse. He fingered the cameo pin at her throat.

Abruptly the man turned back to join his friends, who similarly inspected the passengers' possessions, including the large purple plume on Aunt Emily's hat.

Aunt Emily studied the Indian intently before plucking the feather from the hat and presenting it to the curious man, who'd been stroking it. Pleased, he said, "Thank you. Nice lady. You have big heart. Not forget."

To Sarah's surprise, Emily patted the Indian's arm and said sweetly, "Silver and gold have I none; but such as I have give I thee."

The Indians, prodded by the gunmen and having satisfied their curiosity, mounted their horses and sped away with hoots of laughter——and a purple feather.

Dining at the Dodge House hotel with the other passengers, Sarah found the quiet young man who'd befriended her earlier a talkative, pleasant dinner companion.

"You seem to know much about Indians, eh . . . , Mr. . . ."

"Simon Letchworth, ladies, at your service." He rose and bowed politely.

"We're glad to make your acquaintance, Mr. Letchworth. I'm Sarah Clarke, and this is my great-aunt, Emily Ruggles."

"How do you do," he bowed again and reseated himself briskly. "In response to your statement, Miss Clarke, I'm well acquainted with the Kansas Indians. I've spent most of my life in Topeka. Those Indians—probably Wichita or Pawnee—remind me of the Kaws, who are quite harmless, but often a nuisance. They have a rude habit of walking into the settlers' homes without so much as a knock on the door, because of their inquisitiveness. They beg food and clothing." He shook his head, "It's a shame the way they grovel."

"Are there any *dangerous* Indians nearby?" Sarah widened her eyes inquisitively.

"Yes, indeed. The Comanche and Kiowa aren't far."

Sipping her tea calmly, Aunt Emily asked, "Planning to stay in Dodge City, Mr. Letchworth?"

"Yes, I came to accept a position at the bank."

"You've been here before?" Sarah asked eagerly.

"Yes, quite a few times."

"What is Dodge City like?" Sarah was curious; she had no idea how long they would have to stay.

"It's quiet tonight, but it can change suddenly. Now that the railroad's here, it's a booming cattle town, and when the cattlemen come in, it becomes a dangerous place. It's not a town for unchaperoned ladies to stay in long." Simon leaned over and added in a whisper, "Indeed, even I never venture out when the cattlemen come to town!"

"What do they do?" Sarah tilted her blond head and looked at him with questioning eyes.

"Drink, gamble, and shoot each other, mostly," he answered casually, breaking open a biscuit and smearing it with butter. "How long do you ladies plan on staying?"

"Just until we're contacted. You see," Sarah explained, "I've inherited a ranch in Texas. My grandfather's lawyer plans to meet us here in Dodge City, then escort us to the ranch."

"For your sakes, I hope he arrives soon," Simon warned. "Be sure to check with the desk clerk and post office tomorrow. A message may be waiting for you. We were, after all, delayed several times in our travels."

"I'll do that, sir. Will we be seeing you again?" Sarah asked as Mr. Letchworth stood to depart.

"I usually eat here when in town, so you'll probably see

quite a bit of me. Take care, ladies. I would advise you to go directly to your room and lock the door. Good night." He bowed courteously.

Lying upon her bed that night, Sarah recalled Simon's warning. She was not one to become alarmed easily, but the street noises increasingly made her restless. She shuddered at the sounds of laughter, cursing, and fighting, all amid bawdy dance-hall music from several saloons. Now and then she heard female laughter and wondered what woman dared be with those uncouth men.

Gunshots! The room vibrated with their peals. Sarah gripped the side of her bed, then loudly exhaled the breath she'd been holding and relaxed as loud laughter rang out from the street below. *Oh, what a horrid town! I hope we won't stay long.* Judging from her snores, Emily Ruggles wouldn't lose any sleep no matter where she bedded. Sarah, however, slept lightly.

Quiet came with early morning, and Sarah felt peaceful again, but sleep would not come. Finally she decided to rise and check with the desk to see if the lawyer had left word for her. There was no message there, so she breakfasted with Aunt Emily before venturing to the post office.

Locking Aunt Emily securely in their room, she headed for the front door of the hotel. Sarah stood on the wooden walk, gazing up and down the dusty street, reading the primitive signs: *Long Branch Saloon, Gunsmith and Saddle Shop, Saratoga Saloon, Bank,* and finally the words *Post Office,* written above the door of People's General Store. She hurried in that direction.

The tired-looking storekeeper handed her a letter he said had arrived days ago. She hurried back to the hotel, clutching the envelope excitedly.

Entering the hotel room, Sarah smiled. Aunt Emily calmly sewed, looking as comfortable as if she were in their Chicago sitting room.

"It's here!" Sarah said, waving the envelope. "It's from the lawyer, Samuel Lewis, and it's been here, waiting for us."

"Sit down on the bed and read it to me," Aunt Emily responded without looking up.

Opening the envelope, Sarah read aloud.

April, 1876

Dear Miss Clarke:

I hope your trip was not too unpleasant.

I'm presently in Fort Worth on an important matter and cannot meet you in Dodge City as planned. However, a trustworthy young man, with whom I'm well-acquainted, is traveling to Dodge City on a cattle drive around the time of your arrival. He has most generously agreed to escort you and your aunt safely to Arrow C Ranch. I will contact you when I am able. Everything is in readiness for your arrival.

Your escort, a man named Storm, will call at the hotel when he arrives. Should a problem arise, contact me at the address on the envelope.

Respectfully,
Samuel E. Lewis, Esquire

Sarah handed the letter to Aunt Emily and sighed, "A Mr. Storm is to escort us. I hope he gets here soon. This town unnerves me."

"It seems pleasant enough," Emily commented, skimming the lawyer's letter before putting it aside to continue with her sewing.

"Didn't you hear all the noise last night?"

"Why, no, I slept soundly," Emily replied, biting off her sewing thread.

"I'm glad." Sarah smiled. "What are you mending?"

"Oh, I'm just reinforcing a few seams."

"You needn't bother with that now."

"A stitch in time saves—"

"Nine! I know!" Sarah laughed and embraced the petite, gray-haired woman. How desolate she would feel if Aunt Emily were not with her! Her own mother, currently visiting the spas in Europe, would never have accompanied her to this wild, unpredictable land.

Fondly caressing her aunt's small, blue-veined hand, she sighed. "I wish mother were more like you."

"Your mother is a fine woman."

"Yes, but not spunky and adventurous, like you."

"She never was happy living the hard life. A dreamer, she was. Always imagining that prince who'd wisk her away to his castle."

"And didn't her dream come true when Dad struck gold?"

"Yes, and she had prodded him to go. I remember it like yesterday. It was 1849, and everyone was excited about the gold rush. He was gone three years and came back rich. That was when they moved to Chicago and he went into the newspaper business."

"I never understood why he went back," Sarah said. "They had enough money. Why did he want more gold? He'd be alive today had he stayed home."

"Greed. I don't mean to criticize your folks, but it happens to people sometimes when they have so much. . . . They want more. They began a life-style that was expensive, with friends who had even more than they did."

"Mother never liked to talk about my father's death. Do you know what happened?"

"Not exactly. Just that he and his friends traveled too close to Indians and were attacked. That type of thing happened more often in those days than now."

Sarah had always thought Texas a horrid place. As rich as her father, Thomas Clarke, had become, he had never gone back to his home in Texas and never visited his father, Wilson Clarke. Wilson Clarke had outlived his son by ten

13

years. Sarah wondered how Wilson had taken the news of his only son's death. Had he longed to see him after so many years? She knew they corresponded by mail infrequently, but she had never been invited to read the letters.

Now, here she was, traveling to her own ranch, a legacy from a grandfather she had never met.

Sarah bent to kiss the gently creased but still pretty face of her great-aunt. Traveling to a strange and possibly unwelcome destination, twenty-two-year-old Sarah was often plagued by needling doubts and uncertain fears. Aunt Emily always managed to fortify and strengthen her.

They had recently read an article in the Chicago newspaper about the courageous and persevering Kansas immigrants who had settled and tamed that frontier. Aunt Emily had encouraged her to be like them, to survive, even prosper at running the ranch. Sarah knew the land was cleared and the ranch built. How difficult could it be?

So with Aunt Emily's support Sarah set her mind to overcoming her fears and succeeding as a Texas ranch owner.

Simon Letchworth joined them at dinner, talking incessantly about his new bank position. Unable to believe he'd once been so quiet, Sarah waited for an opportunity to tell their news from Samuel Lewis. When she finally edged it into the conversation, his reply baffled her.

"When your escort comes, *you'll know it!*"

"I will?"

"Certainly. He won't be driving cattle alone. Cattlemen usually travel with numerous cowhands, and sometimes several neighboring ranchers band together to bring their cattle in to be railed. The town will shake from end to end when they arrive, I assure you." Simon patted his mouth with his napkin in a rather feminine way. "You'll know."

"They must have arrived last night then. The noise was unbelievable," Sarah added with a touch of disgust.

"Oh, no. Last night was a normal Friday in Dodge City. You'll know when the cattlemen arrive!" Simon warned. He then chattered about his new job for the rest of the meal.

Sarah finished eating in silence, hardly listening to Simon Letchworth's conversation. She wondered, *How could the cattlemen be any louder than last night's ruckus?*

They came that very night, shortly before dark. To Sarah, at first the uproar sounded like thunder. Then as the hotel began to vibrate, she thought of an earthquake. When she peered out her window and saw an immense cloud of dust moving rapidly toward town, she knew. *The cattlemen!*

She had mixed feelings. While anxious to meet Mr. Storm and be on their way, she dreaded being in the same town with those overzealous cowboys Simon Letchworth had warned about.

"What is it, Sarah?" her aunt asked impatiently

"It's the cattlemen," she answered flatly.

"They certainly know how to make an entrance," Emily said, coming to peek out the window. "Goodness, those cattle have such big horns—ornery looking too."

Later the women wisely stayed away from the window. When the celebration began, men raced their horses through town, shooting their guns at random, whooping and hooting wildly. Until the wee hours of Sunday, the noise of the cattlemen's revelry had to be tolerated.

Sarah could only imagine the activity behind the closed swinging doors of the saloons. Women screamed. Glass shattered. Men shouted and laughed. But the gay piano music stopped only when a fight broke out, and then Sarah could hear cursing, furniture breaking, and gunshots. Then the music would resume in the same lively, carefree manner.

Sleep, for Sarah, came with the sunrise and its accompanying peace. But after only a few hours' slumber someone pounded insistently on her door. Because she wasn't dressed, she called out groggily, "Who's there?"

"Billy O'Hearn, desk clerk. There's a *person* to see Miss Sarah Clarke."

"A person?" she asked.

"He's waitin' outside the hotel. You want I should tell him you'll be down?" the voice asked in an irritated manner.

Sarah decided it best to comply rather than question him further. As she dressed and made a hasty toilet, she wondered at the odd ways of these Kansas people. In the civilized city of Chicago, a caller was always identified as a "lady" or a "gentleman"—never a "person." Unless, of course, she reminded herself, it was a person of low standing, which seldom applied to her family's callers.

After leaving a note for Aunt Emily—who amazed Sarah by sleeping through the pounding on the door—she made her way downstairs. She wondered why the caller didn't meet her in the lobby as was proper protocol.

Clad in a mauve, bustled dress, matching feathered hat, and carrying a white ruffled parasol, Sarah stepped out of the hotel into blinding, midmorning sunlight. Shielding her eyes, she glanced up and down the street, unable to discern anyone looking as if he were waiting for her.

A heavily bearded man loaded a wagon in front of the dry-goods store, but he didn't look her way. Two women chatted near the gunsmith shop, but the clerk had identified her caller as "he." The only other person in sight was a man leaning against the hotel hitching post, with his back to her.

Bewildered, she sighed.

About the time she noticed that the man leaning on the post had unusually long hair, he turned and smiled brightly. *An Indian!* Sarah turned to flee, frightened to her core that he might want to fondle her hair—or worse!

"Miss Clarke?" The voice was smooth, gentlemanly.

Sarah froze in her tracks. She spun around to see if it had indeed been the savage who had addressed her!

Hat in hand, the man stood proudly. Only his eyes pleaded for her attention.

"You wanted to see *me?"* she gasped, too stunned to hide the disgust from her face or tone.

His smile vanished, and he stared blankly.

"My apologies for bothering you," he said, not sounding sorry. "My name is *Storm,* and Sam Lewis said—"

"You are Mr. Storm?" she broke in. "We're supposed to travel safely to the ranch with *you?"* Sarah, surprised with her own rudeness, later excused herself by blaming her behavior on sudden fear and disappointment.

"I'm leaving Friday for Arrow C. If you'd like my escort, be here at dawn," he said, pointing to the wooden walk where they stood.

Sarah spoke politely, already regretting her insolence. "I'm sorry, Mr. Storm, but I cannot accompany you." She avoided looking at him, despite the fact that he wasn't as fearful looking as the Indians who'd stopped their stage. In fact, when she thought about him later, she admitted he was rather handsome—for an Indian!

"You *can't* accompany me, or you *won't?"* he asked, mockingly.

She struggled inwardly then blurted, "Really, Mr. Storm! You—you're an—an—*Indian!"*

"How observant. I assume you have another way of getting to the ranch?" He leaned arrogantly against the post as she faltered for an answer.

Instead of wearing old cast-off clothes as the Indians on the trail had, this man was neatly dressed in dark pants with a blue shirt and leather vest. Only his shoulder-length hair—with a red bandana around his forehead—had alarmed Sarah, identifying him as an Indian.

Sneaking a quick glance at him now, she noted that while he had a dark complexion and high cheekbones, his sensitive eyes were a warm, smoky gray. Had his hair been cut short, she'd not have guessed he was an Indian so quickly. He rather resembled Joe, their Italian iceman from Chicago, except the man before her was more rugged looking.

"Perhaps I'll hire someone or take a stage," she suggested feebly.

"Good luck." He smoothed his hat as he spoke. "If you change your mind, I can be reached through Reverend Thatcher, whose place is behind the blacksmith shop. Good day." The man donned his wide-brimmed hat and walked away without looking back.

Sarah's fear of the man had vanished. His impeccable speech indicated his education and apparent state of being quite civilized. Could she have been too hasty in refusing his escort?

Oh, dear! How would they get to the ranch now?

2

"The only good Indian is a dead Indian. You see, Miss Ruggles," Simon Letchworth smiled at Emily, "I can quote sayings, too!"

"Well then," she said saucily, "how about, 'Judge not, that ye be not judged'?"

"Who said that?" asked Simon. "Not Shakespeare?"

"*God* said that," Aunt Emily snapped with finality.

"It's from the Bible, Mr. Letchworth," Sarah said, though she felt like clapping and yelling "Bravo," for Aunt Emily had bested him. She quickly changed the subject.

"Actually, Mr. Storm *did* seem civilized, and I doubt he's a full-blooded Indian. His eyes are gray, not black like the Indians we met on the trail, and his hair is lighter and—"

"He still can't come into the hotel," Simon cut in. "Indians aren't allowed. Most places in town are barred to even half-breeds. Don't underestimate a half Indian. Quanah Parker, the Comanche chief, is a half-breed and led a raid against white buffalo hunters in Texas a few years ago."

"Many an Englishman killed other Englishmen during the Revolutionary War. American killed American during the Civil War, too," Aunt Emily retorted.

Simon glared at Emily, "A colonel, Chivington I believe, said before going into an Indian battle, 'Kill and scalp all, big and small. Nits make lice!' "

Both women gasped.

Sarah filled their teacups with a shaking hand. "I find that distasteful. While I wouldn't entertain an Indian, I'd not want to see one harmed, especially a child. Surely this colonel joked."

"On the contrary," Simon pushed his empty plate away and reached for his tea. "He was quite serious and proved it during the battle. I'd tell the details, but since you are ladies and dining—"

"Thank you, Mr. Letchworth," Emily interrupted sharply, "for sparing us the gory details. Sarah and I both lost our fathers at the hands of Indians. I believe you are upsetting Sarah with this talk. I had the fortune to live among the Indians in Pennsylvania, after they became peaceful. Sarah has not."

"But Miss Ruggles, it's the truth." Simon peered over his glasses at her. "Indians are brutal savages who kill people by sneaking up on them. You've never seen the remains of a settler's home after an attack. I have. A bloody—"

"Mr. Letchworth," Emily interrupted, "would you like more tea?" When he motioned that he did not, she continued. "The problem is how are we to get to the ranch?"

"We haven't a notion where it is," said Sarah, "except somewhere in northern Texas. Naturally we want to get there as soon as possible . . . yet. . . ." Sarah played with her napkin nervously. "Surely this Mr. Storm is a trustworthy escort. He was recommended by our attorney."

Simon raised his eyebrows dramatically and asked, "But would you sleep at night?"

"Meaning?" Sarah's blue eyes widened.

"Are you sure the half-breed won't attack while you sleep?" Simon sipped his tea daintily. "That's how they operate." His eyes, already magnified by the eyeglasses,

grew even larger as he emphasized, "They creep, they snea.
and they capture—when it's least expected. Gives them the
advantage. No. Better contact your attorney and have him
send someone else to escort you."

"Thank you for your concern, but Sarah and I will make
the decision." Emily Ruggles scowled and rose from the
table. "One must never look a gift horse in the mouth, you
know. Come, Sarah, we've a lot to talk over."

Once safely locked in their room, Aunt Emily suggested
they reread the letter from Mr. Lewis.

Sarah read Mr. Lewis's words aloud. "Well, what do you
think, Aunt Emily?"

Carefully searching the trunk for their nightclothes, Emily
asked, "Where did Mr. Storm say he could be reached?"

"At Reverend Thatcher's, behind the blacksmith shop.
Why?"

"I'm thinking we should send word that we'd be pleased
to have him escort us to the ranch on Friday. After all, Mr.
Lewis claims an acquaintance with this Mr. Storm and
endorses him as trustworthy. If you can't trust your lawyer,
whom can you trust?"

"I agree. I feel less safe here." Sarah shivered.

Pulling Sarah's favorite blue nightgown from the trunk,
Aunt Emily tossed it to her. "Do put out the lamp, Sarah, so
we can undress without all Dodge City watching us."

Sarah snuffed out the kerosene lamp. "There's something
about Mr. Storm I trust; I'm not sure what. . . . But fear
overwhelmed that instinct when I met him today."

"You've always been a good judge of people," Emily said,
climbing into the rickety double bed.

Sarah began her vigorous nightly hair brushing. "Why
should we worry? There are two of us and only one of him."

"He should be worrying!" Aunt Emily quipped. "Remember, Sarah, what the pioneer woman in Lawrence said?
'If you want to survive in this untamed land, you have to be
courageous and determined.' I've two qualities of my own to

d: spirit and grit. And we, my dear, have them all, don't
we?"

"I'd like to think so."

Emily propped herself up on an elbow, "Another thing,
Sarah. We always go to church, though we aren't as close to
God as we should be. We'll add God to our survival list. Now
put that brush down, or you won't have any corn-topped
hair left for the Indians to touch!"

Laughing, Sarah crawled into bed beside her aunt. "You're
right about God, which reminds me of something else. A
man, Indian or otherwise, who is staying with a reverend,
can't be all bad."

"Hm-m-m . . . depends on what kind of reverend he is.
Don't forget to say your prayers, dear." Moments later Sarah
heard her aunt's familiar snoring.

Despite the street noises, Sarah fell asleep soon after but
awoke abruptly long before daylight. A horrid nightmare
held her clammy and breathless. The leather-skinned Indian
from the trail fondled her hair, then her neck. Squeezing her
throat brutally, he laughed in that horrid way he had on the
trail. Then his face changed, and he became Mr. Storm. With
his hands gripping her neck, he asked mockingly, "You *can't*
accompany me or you *won't?*"

She rubbed her throat and reviewed the dream in her
mind. One part struck her as odd. When the man strangling
her had changed from the trail Indian to Mr. Storm, she had
felt relief and a loosening of the hands around her neck. A
sign that Mr. Storm could be trusted? Certainly her dream
implied Mr. Storm was the lesser of the two evils. While not
completely reassuring her, the thought that Mr. Storm might
be trustworthy calmed her.

The next day they sent the message to Mr. Storm. His only
reply was a terse note repeating the order to be ready Friday
at dawn and a list of supplies they would need.

Sarah and Aunt Emily bought bedrolls, sturdy shoes,

sunbonnets, and practical dresses. In his note Mr. Storm emphasized "no bustles or lace."

Friday, in the chill of predawn darkness, they dressed excitedly for their adventure. Sarah, still fashion minded, chose a light-blue homespun with high neck and long, cuffed sleeves. Aunt Emily carefully brushed Sarah's thick, golden hair, arranging it beneath her sunbonnet so that the curls peeked out smartly in just the right places.

Studying herself in the small bureau mirror, Sarah adjusted her white bonnet and giggled.

"Aunt Emily! What would Clarence Van Meter think if he could see me now? Or Charles Southwick? Wouldn't Minerva Farnsworth love to see me at one of her teas, wearing this?"

Adjusting Sarah's bonnet, Aunt Emily said, "You look lovely. Those Chicago men would see your beauty shining through even this plain outfit. It's your smooth, rosy complexion and bright-blue eyes, always wide with excitement, that make you attractive, not bustles and silks. Beauty is only skin deep you know! Besides, your sparkling vitality and warmth keep the bees at the nest, once they're attracted by the honey."

Sarah laughed.

"Thank you, Aunt Emily, nothing could boost my morale more. But will we ever get to wear our city clothes again?"

Emily pinched Sarah's cheek playfully. "Once we get to your ranch, I imagine we can dress any way we please."

Pink slivers of light had barely sliced into the dark eastern sky when Mr. Storm drew up at the hotel in a buckboard pulled by two stout oxen.

After easing their heavy trunk onto the back of the wagon, he helped the ladies up onto the driver's bench, placing Sarah between himself and Aunt Emily. Silently they rode down the quiet, deserted street.

they traveled, the sun rose steadily, giving Sarah a
ter view of Mr. Storm. He'd gotten a haircut! While
horter, his dark hair still covered most of his ears. If he had
it cut on her account, to lessen her fright, he'd succeeded. He
didn't look quite so "Indian" with the new cropped hair.

Caught in the act of scrutinizing him, she asked quickly,
"Why have we oxen pulling the wagon, instead of horses?"

With tightened lips, he replied almost reluctantly, "The
wagon's carrying a heavy load, and it's a long way to Texas."
He glanced at her briefly before continuing, with a bit more
enthusiasm, "Oxen are the best choice for this type of
journey. They make the numerous river crossings better and
aren't skittish. They don't tire as easily as horses either."

"If something happened to one of them, could the other
pull alone?" she asked.

"We have extra oxen, just in case. Cattlemen never travel
without extra mounts and teams."

"Where are they?" she asked, turning to look behind
them.

"Up ahead. My outfit is waiting for us south of the city."
He looked at her intently, then laughed. "Surely you didn't
think we were on our way with just us and this wagon?"

Sarah didn't answer. Confused at his words and annoyed
by his laughter, her face flushed. With trembling lips she
fought to control her emotions.

They turned onto a narrow dirt road leading south, and he
pointed ahead. "There's our crew!"

Sarah gasped, unable to believe her eyes.

Halting the team, he looked at her oddly. "Is there a
problem?"

"B-but they're all *Indians!*" she stammered, grabbing Aunt
Emily's arm for support. She couldn't believe they would be
traveling with not one, but almost a *dozen* Indians! She
turned to Mr. Storm for reassurance but saw only amusement
on his face. He seemed to be enjoying her discomfort.

Aunt Emily squeezed her hand and whispered softly,

"Remember, dear, courage, determination, spirit, grit, a
God."

Sarah raised her chin proudly and straightened her back.
She would not give Mr. Storm the satisfaction of knowing
how frightened or uncomfortable the situation made her.
She'd prove she possessed the qualities needed to succeed in
Texas.

"Actually," Mr. Storm said, as if finally feeling some
sympathy for her, "they aren't *all* Indians."

"No?" Sarah asked quickly.

"Certainly not. Emmanuel, our head cook, is Mexican. We
call him Manny. That's him leaning against the chuck
wagon."

Sarah followed his pointed finger to a graying, mustached
man lounging against a covered wagon. As they gazed
Manny nodded and tipped his large-brimmed hat respectfully.

"See the man checking the ox halter?" Storm pointed
again. "That's Leo. As you can see he's a Negro. Does your
prejudice include Mexicans and Negroes, Miss Clarke? No, I
can see not, just Indians."

Sarah, too stunned to comment, stared at him in disbelief.

"I suppose you're anxious to begin. I'll find you a driver,"
he said jumping from the wagon.

"Find a driver? Wait . . . , Mr. Storm!" she cried, already
forgetting her brave resolution.

He swung around angrily, yet spoke softly, "One favor,
Miss Clarke, don't call me 'Mister'; my men will find that too
amusing. At least around them—it's Storm, just Storm "

"All right then, er, Storm. Aren't *you* going to drive our
wagon?"

"Can't. I'm trail boss and must ride about. I'll be back now
and then to check on you, but I have a job to do."

"Will we be able to. . . ? I mean, can we t-trust . . . ?" she
faltered.

"All my men are hand selected by me, and I was trusted by

grandfather. Therefore, rest assured that anyone I
oose will be above reproach." He turned and headed
wiftly toward his men.

"He's right, dear," comforted Aunt Emily. "And a fine lad!
I trust him completely." She chuckled before quoting, "The
lion is not so fierce as he is painted."

"Aunt Emily, you've only known him ten minutes!"

"Yes, but he reminds me of Finney Horrigan. You wouldn't
know Finney," she continued in a reminiscent tone. "He was
a special friend back in Uniontown."

"Were you in love with Finney?" Sarah asked. "I didn't
know about anyone special in your life."

"I'll tell you about Finney someday. He was very special,
and Mr. Storm reminds me of Finney, so I know he can be
trusted."

Sarah watched Storm standing by the two canvas-covered
wagons, conversing with his men. A large herd of horses
pranced energetically within a roped area, and four muscular
oxen grazed nearby.

Storm returned moments later with a short, bowlegged
Indian.

"Miss Clarke, Miss Ruggles, may I present your driver,
Hunter," he introduced royally.

Sarah studied the older man, noting the deep, meaningful
lines engraved into his face. Nodding, Hunter lithely jumped
onto the driver's bench beside Sarah.

Storm, noticing Sarah's edging away from touching the
Indian, sauntered over to the ladies' side of the wagon.
Gazing steadily in Sarah's eyes (which she knew must have
resembled a cornered rabbit's, darting apprehensively from
Storm to Hunter), he frowned.

"Trust me, ladies," Storm reassured. "Hunter is my uncle,
my mother's brother."

Sarah glanced at Hunter, who grinned widely at her. She
returned the smile hesitantly, which seemed to satisfy Storm.

Aunt Emily leaned over Sarah. "Any uncle of Storm's friend of ours. Welcome, Hunter."

Storm thanked Aunt Emily, then addressed both women. "See the man soothing the horses? That's Broken Wing. He broke his arm severely as a child. It's completely useless now. Yet he is an important member of the crew. As an animal lover he has a unique way with them. Often, when spooked by noises, the longhorns become restless, and stampede—the greatest threat to bringing cattle in to be railed. Stampedes are not only destructive but time consuming, for the cattle must all be rounded up again afterward.

"On the trail, Broken Wing sleeps near the cattle, soothing them when they become fidgety. We haven't had a stampede since he's been with us. He also tames wild horses, and ranchers travel miles to have theirs broken by him."

"Broken?" Sarah asked.

"Tamed so they can be saddled and ridden."

Storm pointed again, "There's Leo. He was a slave back in Alabama but can't speak to you. His white master clipped his tongue for talking back to a white woman who was verbally abusing him publicly.

"The man beside him is Red Moon, an Indian school graduate and the only crew member, besides Manny, who can read and write.

"As we travel, I hope you'll become better acquainted with them." Storm looked directly at Sarah. "Perhaps, when you know each individually, you'll realize that despite being different, they're people, just like you."

Storm returned to his men, and within minutes their small wagon train began its procession southward, toward Texas. Storm had positioned their wagon ahead of the supply wagon and animal herd. Later Sarah discovered that the chuck wagon and Storm rode far ahead so that after camping where Storm directed, the food would be ready by the time the rest arrived.

Though the trail became bumpy and the weather hot,

ah and Aunt Emily agreed it was an improvement from e crowded, fast-moving stagecoach. The oxen traveled more slowly, enabling them the pleasure of viewing the outdoors and watching the beauty of nature around them.

They eagerly identified the various bird calls and became enthralled by the occasional critter scurrying into the bush along the trail.

Hunter, noticing this, went out of his way to point these things out for them. He'd simply point and grunt, then smile widely at the women's pleasure over the squirrel or raccoon he'd brought to their attention.

Not long before noon that first day on the trail, Storm rode back to point out a small group of antelope grazing on the open prairie.

As they watched, Hunter slipped from his seat and carefully stalked them with his bow and arrow. Sarah saw him silently slip from bush to bush. It wasn't until he'd sprung his large bow that the animals knew of his presence. But too late. Hunter's arrow, skillfully launched, plunged deeply into the heart of one large buck. Springing to run, it stopped abruptly before dropping heavily to the ground, while its friends loped off toward a small wooded area.

"Well, ladies, looks like fresh meat for supper!" Storm announced. "Need I tell you how Hunter got his name?" He added, "We'll stop here for a cold lunch. We only build a fire for the evening meal."

The meal consisted of biscuits and cheese. They drank a measured amount of water from a large barrel, which Sarah thought the best she'd ever tasted. Thirstier than she could ever recall being but not offered seconds of the water, she approached Storm and demanded to know why they were denied more.

He gave her a sympathetic look, then sadly glanced down at his own newly poured cup before resolutely handing it to her. She drank it slowly, savoring every drop. When she finished, he explained.

"Our water supply is limited to what's in these two barrels," he said pointing to the supply wagon. "We filled them to the brim in Dodge, from the Arkansas River. There isn't another drop of water until we reach the Cimarron River, which is about sixty miles, or four days away."

"Oh," was Sarah's only reply. She looked down at his empty cup in her hand. His ration! How foolish she had been. She lowered her eyes shamefully, but her look was misinterpreted.

"And don't feel sorry for yourself," he said firmly yet kindly, as if to a child. "Though rationed, you'll get your share of water, while these poor animals doing all the work in this heat, will not."

"Not any?" she asked, feeling instantly sorry for the livestock.

"Not one drop. If we don't reach the Cimarron in four days some will likely die."

Embarrassingly satisfied, Sarah did not complain again about the rationed water but wondered about the half-Indian man who had given her his share of water after working hard in the hot sun and dust.

Sarah and Emily stretched their legs, freshened themselves, and took a brisk walk before returning to their seat on the wagon. Now appreciative of their solid walking shoes, cotton dresses, and bonnets, Sarah realized why Storm had insisted on them. They wouldn't have lasted a day in the Chicago finery.

That first night Sarah managed to further annoy Storm. Sitting around the fire that evening, feasting on roasted venison, Sarah was shocked by the Indians' primitive eating habits. She picked up her plate and slipped away, perching herself on a large rock some distance from the others.

"What did you expect, Miss Clarke, a tablecloth and silverware?" Storm startled her by speaking close behind her.

She jumped, then blurted, "Why do they eat with their fingers? It's disgusting!"

"Those Indians have come a long way since coming to the ranch." Storm, also with plate in hand, squatted beside her. "I'd hate them to think you didn't like or approve of them. Knowing you're the new boss, they are quite anxious to please and concerned about your opinion of them."

"They are? I never thought of them as being sensitive." Sarah paused, eyeing him carefully. "I notice you're using a fork—couldn't you teach them?"

"I've taught them a great deal, but still have a long way to go." He laughed. "You're lucky they're wearing clothes!" At her puzzled start, he explained. "When some first came to the ranch they wore only . . . well, very little."

Sarah blushed at the mention of the barely clad Indians and quickly changed the subject.

"Tell me about my grandfather's ranch."

Storm set down his empty plate, "What do you want to know?"

"Where is it? How long before we get there?"

"Arrow C is near the Red River, which separates Oklahoma from Texas. We should reach the river in three weeks to a month's time. From Doan's Crossing it's only a five-hour ride to the ranch."

Sarah drew lines in the dust with a small stick. "I never knew my grandfather. What was he like?"

"Wilson Clarke was an extraordinary man." Storm said brusquely.

"You were good friends?" she asked.

He said nothing for so long Sarah feared he hadn't heard her. "You might say that," he mumbled finally. Standing, he brushed the dust from his trousers and leaned against the rock she sat upon.

"You would have liked him."

She smiled. "Do you live near the ranch?"

"I thought you knew I live *on* the ranch and have since before your grandfather died. What I do now, of course, depends on you." He paused. "There's something else you should know. I'm hoping you'll get over your aversion to Indians before we reach Arrow C, because my mother lives there, too. I won't have her feelings hurt, Miss Clarke, by you or anyone." His voice left no doubt that he meant what he said.

"I didn't know." Sarah whispered softly, as if in reverence to his mother. "How did she come to live there with you?"

"It's a long story, but I'll condense it. My mother, Red Dawn—called Dawn—came to the ranch as a young girl. Your grandfather hired Indians whenever he could, not only because he liked them, but because they protected his ranch from Indian raids. My mother was hired as housekeeper and has been there ever since.

"Having always been a favorite of Wilson's, she is treated like family." He glared at her intently. "I hope you will treat her kindly as well."

The thought of living in the same house with an Indian— male or female—made Sarah uneasy. She said nothing to reassure Storm but soon wished she had, for he turned abruptly and left her alone to ponder the problem.

That night Sarah slept beneath the stars for the first time. She and Aunt Emily were placed on the opposite side of the fire from the men.

As usual, Aunt Emily's snores sounded long before Sarah even got comfortable in her bedroll. Sarah tossed and turned. She kept hearing Simon Letchworth's words, ". . . But would you sleep? . . . Indians are nothing but brutal savages who kill people by sneaking up on them. . . . They creep, they sneak, and they capture. . . ."

Listening to the hooting owls and howling animals, Sarah watched the Indian on guard poke playfully at the fire then

31

realized a full bladder summoned her to the woods, despite her trip there earlier with Aunt Emily. Not knowing what to do, she tried to ignore the uncomfortable pressure. Rather than awaken Aunt Emily, she reluctantly tiptoed into the dark night alone, clutching a light shawl around her shoulders.

Sarah stumbled blindly into the practically moonless night. An animal howled nearby; she quivered, tightening her shawl about her.

She'd nearly reached the large clump of bushes when an arm sprung out, grabbing her waist from behind, while a strong hand clamped tightly over her mouth. Eyes wide with fear, Sarah struggled wildly to free herself, but to no avail.

A deep voice whispered hoarsely but softly in her ear. "Stop fighting me!"

～ 3 ～

"*S*top fighting me," the voice repeated. "It's Storm." He slowly removed his hand from her mouth.

Sarah spun around. "Why did you grab me? You scared me to—"

"Sh-h-h," he whispered. "You'll wake the whole crew. Why are you wandering around alone at night?" he demanded.

"I had to . . . nature called." She mumbled, thankful for the darkness that hid her blush.

"I grabbed you so you wouldn't scream and wake everyone!" he growled. "I can't have you marching around alone in such dangerous territory! If you knew some of the things that could happen, you'd be more frightened than you were just now." As if suddenly conscious of their closeness, he took a step backwards.

"Next time tell me when nature calls. I or someone will walk with you. This is no place for modesty. Now go and attend to whatever you must, but if you need me, holler." Storm stretched out on a grassy mound nearby, "I'll wait right here."

33

Completing her task, Sarah returned to where he waited and hesitantly sat down beside him.

"I'm sorry for being such a nuisance. I couldn't sleep."

"You'll get used to camping." He studied her face in the dim moonlight. "Or is it something else that causes you to lose sleep? Like the company you're keeping?"

Sarah sat speechless. He was certainly perceptive. Finally she whispered, "Can you assure me Indians are completely harmless?"

"Certainly not. Some Indians are still dangerous, but so are a good number of white men. Is it sensible to chastise a whole race for the acts of a few? Indians are hurt and confused right now. They've had . . . well, I won't go into that now."

Storm sighed impatiently. "Would Sam Lewis send a pack of dangerous savages to escort you? And if you can't trust Lewis, surely you can trust your grandfather."

He stood and reached for her hand. "I'd better walk you back to camp."

After helping her stand, he dropped her hand as though it were something forbidden.

Surprisingly, his touch hadn't repulsed her as she had imagined physical contact with an Indian would. She shivered, remembering the crude fondling of the bold Indian from the trail.

Storm led her back to the fire and ordered her into her bedroll. She obeyed.

Positioning himself cross-legged on the ground near her feet, he hesitated and studied her face carefully.

"I-I'm only half Indian."

Suddenly it became too quiet. Even the crackling of the fire seemed muted. She glanced at him. His sad face glowed from the flickering fire, and his worried eyes danced with orange flames.

"I guessed that."

"Does that make you any less afraid of me?"

"Yes," she grinned, propping herself on one elbow. "You're only half as savage looking as the Indians who chased our stagecoach in Kansas."

"You were attacked on the trail?" he asked in disbelief.

"Oh, no. We thought they were attacking, but actually they acted out of curiosity. I must admit though, I was terrified at the time. One savage insisted on touching my hair, calling me 'corn-topped lady'! Some women in Topeka had related tales about Indians that would have frightened anyone! And my father was killed by Indians—"

"No wonder the sight of me in Dodge shocked you," he sympathized. "Your grandfather never told me how your father died. I'm sorry." He gazed at her tenderly for several moments before whispering, "Lie down, try to relax and sleep. You have nothing to fear; Sarah." His voice was gentle and reassuring. "I'll sit here until you're asleep. My own bedroll is nearby."

Eyes growing heavy from extreme fatigue, Sarah finally relaxed. All the sleepless nights of the past weeks had finally caught up with her. Storm's presence calmed her fears and gave her mind the peace needed to fall deeply asleep. But before yielding up her awareness, she smiled. He had just called her Sarah for the first time. Had she imagined it, or had he murmured, "You're perfectly safe with me, Sarah, I promise. I'd not let anything happen to you. Trust me"?

For the first time since leaving Chicago Sarah slept soundly, so soundly that she was reluctant to surface, despite someone's constant proddings. She reveled in the cozy depths of slumber where no problems, fears, or anxieties existed. It felt good. Too good. She hated to depart from it.

Yet someone insisted she leave her secure world of dark serenity.

won't respond to the prodding, but why do they persist—king me harder?

"Go away," she mumbled. Her mind quickly attempted to spin back into the dense, dark tunnel of slumber.

Who is it? Why do you shake me? I'm so happy where I am—let me be.

Good. They stopped shaking me, I can delve deeper. . . .

Now what? Someone is . . . caressing my hair. The rude Indian? Alarm almost drew her from her cocoon. *No, the touch is tender—not the savage. The tenderness of the touch conveys caring. Oh, how I need that!*

But the hair caressing stopped. She missed it.

Now someone is stroking my cheek, adoringly. The touch is loving, meaningful, and I'm responding strangely. This sensation is better than the pleasurable sleep. Now I want to awaken, to open my eyes and see who is stirring me.

Purposefully, she opened her bright-blue eyes and met the tenderest smoky-gray ones. Storm. His eyes, while soft, held a sense of urgency or pleading. Was she still asleep? The stroking of her hair and cheek had ceased, yet she still responded. Was she stirred by the tender, vulnerable look on Storm's face?

Sarah blinked. His soul-stirring expression had vanished.

Storm sprang to his feet, "We're breaking camp." He spoke with a soft gruffness, and the sudden change made her shiver. "Thought we'd have to leave you here," he continued. "Do you always sleep so soundly?"

"But it's still dark!" she complained, drawing her blanket over her head.

"We must leave at the first hint of daylight to make the Cimarron in four days," he said briskly. "This isn't a leisurely pleasure trip. We have limited supplies and many dangers. The more time it takes you to get up, the less time you'll have to prepare for the day. In fact, I'd say you had only about fifteen minutes."

Sarah sprang up. "But it will take me at least an hour!"

"We're leaving in fifteen minutes, whether you're ready or not. Of course, if you wish to stay, take your time." He strolled away calmly but too swiftly to hear the words she had aimed at him.

Sarah never moved so fast! The thought of being left behind spurred her into action. Aunt Emily and her bedroll were missing.

How can I dress and arrange my hair without Aunt Emily's help? Should I wear this same wrinkled dress another day? Why did I sleep so long? she asked herself as she rolled up her bedding.

"Sarah, I'm glad you're up!"

"Oh, Aunt Emily!" Sarah exclaimed in relief, then began throwing questions. "Where were you? Why didn't you wake me? Will you help me change? Will you do my hair? What have you there?"

"Breakfast. But it can wait. I'll put it in the wagon. We have to get you ready, fast. I'll answer your other questions while I work."

Grabbing clean clothing, Aunt Emily pulled Sarah into the bushes, talking the whole time.

"I got up early and helped at the chuck wagon; the only way to get decent food, I figured. They loved my griddle cakes. Wait until we get to the ranch and I make my jams! I love cooking for people who appreciate my effort! I rather like them. Don't you? Lift your hair higher, Sarah, I can't hook your dress.

"Sorry, dear, we haven't time to curl and ribbon your hair. Let's just tie it back, like I did mine." Emily pulled back Sarah's long, thick, blond waves and tied them loosely at her neck.

Sarah and her aunt barely made it to the wagon before it jerked forward. Sarah wondered if Storm really would have left her behind, had she not been ready.

Their second day on the trail was uneventful. Storm didn't reappear until they made camp that night. He nodded briefly her direction, then busied himself at the horse corral the whole evening.

Storm's aloofness first angered Sarah, but soon the anger turned to loneliness. Aunt Emily seemed to always be somewhere else. Sarah needed Storm's friendship and even craved it.

Her loneliness led her to make a decision. She wanted to please Storm, and she needed friends. If she made an effort toward getting along with the Indians, she would solve both problems.

So far, the crew had stayed out of her way, although she often caught them staring at her from a distance. She ate supper that night with them, despite their uncouth table manners.

Aunt Emily helped Manny at the chuck wagon, so Sarah sat on her bedroll beside the wagon and ate. The stew tasted good, and she recognized Aunt Emily's special gravy.

When finished, she set her plate down and daydreamed, staring lazily into space until a shadow crossed in front of her.

Startled, Sarah jumped up.

"I play? You like?"

She sighed softly. It was only one of the Indians holding a pipelike instrument. Hesitantly, she smiled. He put the instrument to his mouth, and beautiful sounds emitted from it. Smiling widely to show her pleasure in the music, Sarah sat down again.

Hunter joined her. By now she was used to his company, having ridden beside him for two days. Beginning to like him, she welcomed him warmly.

"That is Lazy Dog," he nodded toward the young musician. "He used to be called Slow Fire, but because he sits around making much music and no work, we now call him Lazy Dog. Sometimes just Dog!"

"His music is strange, but I like it. What is he playing?"

"A whistle, made from bird bones. Just hope he does not sing."

"Why? Does he sing badly?" she asked.

"Like a dog howling at the moon!" laughed Hunter.

Sarah found herself laughing, too. Then she pointed to an Indian she'd caught staring at her several times before. She had also noticed him as the only crew member with long hair. Was it just the frightening hair, or did she sense this Indian's hostility toward her?

"Who's that?"

"That is Black Feather. He is new. This is his first cattle drive. He is Little Bird's brother."

"Who is Little Bird?"

"Little Bird works at the ranch," he explained.

"See that man there by the fire?" He pointed to an Indian in a bright-red shirt. "That is my son!" he said proudly. "That is Dull Knife. Used to be Young Hunter, but he always forgets to sharpen his knife—so we named him Dull Knife."

"Does everyone change names whenever they want?" she asked.

"You are called what fits—sometimes others name you! It is better to pick a name yourself," he laughed. "One Indian met a skunk in woods—they called him Stinking Dog!" Slapping his knee, he hooted in laughter, until Sarah became caught up in it.

"Is he still called Stinking Dog?" she asked, her eyes tearing from gaiety.

Between howls of uncontrollable laughter, he managed to exclaim, "No, now he is called Hunter!" As Sarah burst into renewed laughter, she realized she was having a good time—with an Indian!

When Aunt Emily and Manny joined them, they moved to the fire, where Manny and Hunter told stories of previous cattle drives. Sarah liked Manny's tale about accidentally putting hot pepper in the stew. He laughed that they were all "on fire," from every end, for three days!

Storm was still absent when she and Emily unrolled their beds. They talked softly for a while; then—practically in midsentence—Aunt Emily began to snore loudly. Alone, Sarah lay silently, unable to relax amid the strange surroundings and wild noises.

Then she spotted Storm. He threw down his bedroll not five feet from her and Aunt Emily. Watching until he disappeared under his blankets, she finally relaxed and fell asleep.

Their daily travel soon became routine, and Sarah noted the constantly changing scenery. Since the day Hunter had killed the antelope, the sight of animals and green wooded areas had vanished. The land had become sandy and dry, the trail hard, unyielding, and dusty.

She yearned for more than the usual ration of water, until she noticed the livestock had become sluggish and slow from lack of any moisture at all. Sarah felt sure the poor animals would soon drop from exhaustion and thirst. She and Emily tried to lighten the oxen's burden by walking alongside the wagon occasionally.

One day the animals perked up somewhat, and with bristled ears and twitching noses they seemed to pick up speed. Hunter explained that they must be close to the Cimarron, for the animals could sense the nearness of water.

Reaching the river midafternoon of the fourth day, Storm permitted them to stay until the following morning, giving them the longest camp yet. He also allowed them to bathe, and the ladies, having never been without water before, couldn't seem to get enough of it.

The land gradually changed from arid desert grassland to lush grassy areas with intermittent woodlands. Once again, they spotted antelope, and Hunter had pointed out a fox, but neither lady had been quick enough to see it.

Storm announced their position as a few miles into the Oklahoma Territory and that from then on water would be plentiful and rationing unnecessary.

Several days after leaving the Cimarron River, the land gradually changed again, to dry, almost desertlike sand. Storm said they traveled just east of No Man's Land in the northern Oklahoma Territory. The land became barren and practically treeless as well. Firewood became a rare commodity.

Already the day was hot. The air hung heavy and dusty, with not even a hint of a breeze to look forward to.

Aunt Emily had asked Sarah to help collect firewood by walking a few miles alongside the wagon. Sarah welcomed the respite, for it felt good to be off one part of the body and onto another.

Upon seeing a stick, they'd snatch it and toss it into the wagon bed.

Hunter pointed out buffalo chips, explaining their usefulness as fuel. While they saw no buffalo, their chips were more easily found than sticks. Sarah felt reluctant to touch them with her hands, until Aunt Emily showed her how dry they were.

Definitely not the same person Sarah remembered from Chicago, Aunt Emily seemed to be having the time of her life. In the city she had seemed every bit her sixty years, while here she flitted about like forty! The West had rejuvenated her, or perhaps it was the adventure. Whatever had caused it, she became a source of constant amazement to Sarah.

Sarah wondered what her mother would think if she could see them now, dressed like settlers, with dusty shoes and smudged faces—picking up sticks *and buffalo chips!* Giggling softly to herself, she pictured her mother's reaction. She loved her mother dearly but knew she'd never approve.

Sarah watched Aunt Emily's little form bouncing along the trail, picking up sticks and chips. How vibrant and alive she was! She hoped with all her being that Aunt Emily found the adventure of her life in Texas. She deserved it.

Sarah spied a stick showing from behind a large rock. She reached down and took hold of it—and its warm, dry, scaliness moved in her hand. Realizing it was alive, she dropped it hastily with a scream, then started to run quickly, too quickly, and tripped over the rock.

Sprawled on the ground, Sarah glanced up to see Dull Knife running toward her. He yelled wildly in a language she didn't understand. A noise like vibrating pebbles sang through the air. She glanced around quickly, trying to identify the sound.

Too late! The snake arched and sprang, striking her in the calf of her left leg. Again Sarah screamed.

Had she screamed yet again? She couldn't be sure. She heard the sound; it could have been her voice, but she didn't think she had the strength to make a sound—especially one so loud and shrill.

Everything seemed hazy. Dizziness overcame her.

No! I never faint—this can't be happening to me.

The next thing she knew, Aunt Emily had appeared and waved a vial beneath her nose. The others surrounded her, looking on in silent wonder.

Sitting up, Sarah pushed the vial away. "I'm all right," she panted, despite her dizziness.

But Dull Knife still frantically muttered words she couldn't understand. She didn't know what he said, but the other Indians did. Wide-eyed, they shook their heads sadly.

One of the Indians, Sarah wasn't sure which, fired his gun at something beyond her. Or she wondered, had he aimed at her and missed?

Sarah tried to stand, but Dull Knife pushed her gently back

down into the dust. Still chattering in the foreign tongue, he unsheathed his knife. Seeing the raised blade in his hand and the savage look on his face, she screamed shrilly. The others quickly grabbed her thrashing limbs, hindering her frantic struggle.

Sarah groaned helplessly. Her worst fears had materialized. She was about to be scalped by Indians!

⚬ 4 ⚬

With knife poised, glinting in the sun, Dull Knife hesitated. Frozen with fear, Sarah stared apprehensively. Had her screams stunned him? Was that a flash of tenderness in his black, darting eyes? No. His hand came down, piercing her skin. Blood oozed from the wound. He cut not her scalp, but her leg, twice.

Sarah, too terror stricken to cry, scream, or speak, watched Dull Knife with wide, horror-filled eyes. Putting his mouth to her wound, he sucked the blood, then spit it out, repeatedly.

Feverishly, she wondered if this were some primitive tribal ceremony performed before taking the scalp. The others looked on in wide-eyed silence, while she battled dizziness, nausea, and anxiety.

Suddenly the crew surrounding her stirred. Someone burst through the circle of men. Storm! Sarah sighed in relief. He would save her!

But no! He slapped Dull Knife's back, "Good work, Dull Knife!"

As she began to slip from consciousness, Aunt Emily waved the vial beneath her nose.

"No!" A revived Sarah cried. "Storm, not you! I trusted you!"

Storm dropped to his knees beside her.

"Please," she cried. "Don't scalp me!"

Storm took her hand. "Sarah, you're hysterical." Beneath his breath he muttered, "Lord, help her, she's in shock." He bent to speak near her ear. "No one is going to scalp or kill you. Oh, Sarah, if this weren't so serious, I'd laugh. Dull Knife just saved your life!

"Hunter grabbed a horse and found me," he explained. "Luckily I wasn't far ahead. I prayed as I sped back, knowing I'd be too late. Which is why I was so relieved to see Dull Knife sucking out the poison." Storm's voice broke with emotion. "If he was fast and thorough enough—you'll—you'll live."

Sarah's eyes flew to Dull Knife, who still labored at removing the venom from her leg. He stopped, and their eyes met.

"Thank you, Dull Knife," she murmured before finally losing consciousness.

When next she opened her eyes, Storm and Aunt Emily, seated wearily at her bedside, were immediately alert. They stared at her expectantly. She smiled. Both let out sighs of relief Sarah was certain could be heard in Chicago!

Aunt Emily hurried away, mumbling something about getting fresh water. Storm still held her hand in his, and when his grip suddenly tightened, she turned to look at him. His eyes were closed and his lips moved, but she heard not a word of his silent conversation, and soon she fell into a restful sleep.

When Sarah awoke, Storm was gone. She sat and let Aunt Emily spoon broth into her mouth. She felt exhausted and weak but wondrously alive! The warm, salty broth was tasty, and she finished it, leaving not a drop. Aunt Emily, pleased with her patient, washed her, groomed her, and helped her into a clean dress. Sarah thanked her.

Patting her hand affectionately, Aunt Emily spoke of the accident for the first time. "My dear, sweet Sarah, I'm just glad you're alive and well for me to fuss over. I couldn't love you more if you were my own daughter. I thrive on our relationship. I'd never have forgiven myself if . . . ," she sniffed into her wrinkled, recently much-used-looking handkerchief.

"And I love you," Sarah said, smiling weakly. "But it was my own fault. How many times had Storm and Hunter warned me about snakes? Life is so different here. Will I ever get used to it?"

"Certainly, we both will." She straightened her back and put on her brave frontier-woman look. "Now, try to sleep. It's what you need most, you know." Emily winked and silently left the small makeshift tent the men had constructed.

Sarah tried to remember all that had happened since the snakebite, but most was hazy, except Aunt Emily and Storm's presence throughout. Squeezing her memory, she recalled thrashing feverishly and deliriously and Aunt Emily's worried clucking as she quenched Sarah's thirst with a wet cloth.

But most vivid was the memory of Storm's strong hand over hers, encouraging her fight for life.

Throughout her struggle, she had fluctuated between sleeping and restless wakefulness—of which she recalled little. Only one memory shone through, and Sarah gave it credit for her fast recovery.

During the peak of her fever, when she'd burned up unbearably and the nausea had become so agonizing, she had uncontrollably cried out for home. Never had she felt so ill. She craved Chicago, her mother's secure arms, and her nanny's strong, sure nursing hands. The man holding her hand had squeezed it hard at her outcry.

"No!" he'd insisted. "You can't give up and go home!"

"I want to go home!" she'd cried, twisting in her sweat-soaked bedroll.

"No!" His voice was firm and authoritative. "We need you. You're going to get well. There's a ranch waiting that needs you!"

"Please! No! Take me home!" she'd pleaded. "I don't like it here. I'm frightened and alone." Clawing blindly at him, she'd begged hysterically, "Please, don't let me die here!"

"Stop, Sarah!" He caught her thrashing hands in his. "You have Aunt Emily, you have God, and you have me! We're all here and care, care very much," he soothed. "Don't you trust me yet?" he had asked with tired exasperation.

She remembered how her feverish eyes had sought his and found trustfulness and caring.

Vaguely she recalled answering with relief, "Yes, I do trust you!"

Tired from straining her memory yet relaxed by its comfort, she fell into restful slumber.

When Sarah awoke, Storm was sitting cross-legged on the ground beside her bedroll.

"You gave us all a scare," he whispered.

"Again, I apologize. I'm causing a great deal of trouble."

"Dull Knife doesn't think so. He boasts a new name and is thrilled with it," Storm said with twinkling eyes.

"What is it?"

"Snakebite!"

She laughed. "And he likes the name?"

"He's the proudest man I've ever seen."

Sarah stopped laughing and became thoughtful. "Storm. . . ."

He looked at her expectantly.

"I'm sorry for something else. I wasn't fair to you or the entire race of Indians. I'm proud to have so many of them for friends. The odd part is, I felt that way before Dull—I mean Snakebite—saved my life. I'm especially glad about that."

Seeing his understanding grin, she continued. "I discovered their friendship one lonely night. Lazy Dog played an instrument for me, Hunter and Manny told stories about previous cattle drives. We sat around the fire and laughed together. I forgot I was with Indians."

"Does it matter *when* you came to your senses?"

"Yes. It's important. Otherwise I would always wonder if my change of feelings were only due to an Indian's saving my life. While I'm extremely grateful, it wasn't what caused my change of heart. I found friends. I came to my own realization that they are living, breathing, caring people."

Storm's eyes softened, "I'm proud of you, Sarah. You've come a long way since you blanched at the sight of me outside the hotel in Dodge City."

"I . . . ," she started.

He held up his hand. "Stop! No apologies necessary. You've said it all. Now let's get down to business.

"We've lost a day on the trail. I talked to the crew, and we decided since you're so much better we'll continue first thing in the morning." She started to speak, but he silenced her again.

"Now, wait. Before you say anything, let me explain what we've decided. A bed will be made on the back of your wagon, and you're to remain in that bed the whole day, or we don't leave. And that could be dangerous to us all." He stood then, brushing the dust from his trousers.

"How can I ever thank you for treating me with such kindness?"

"By being a good and obedient patient." He winked and was gone before she could ask another question.

The next day, as she traveled upon her mobile bed, every member of the outfit came to visit, bearing a gift. Even Black Feather, whom she suspected didn't like her, came with his offering, a robin's egg. He said little, leaving Sarah with the impression he still resented her.

Strangely, they were no longer just Indians or the crew, but individuals. Sarah met gentle Broken Wing; silent, strong Leo; shy Red Moon; comical Little Hawk; talkative Bent Arrow; and ever-complaining but sensitive Eagle Eyes. She received gifts of flowers, birds' eggs, food smuggled from the chuck wagon, a bird feather, and even an arrowhead.

Lazy Dog and Snakebite gathered enough sticks and buffalo chips to last days. They made her promise never to collect firewood again.

Sarah's heart ballooned with love for these people who had frightened her so at first. They laughed now at how she'd thought Snakebite was going to scalp her.

Everyone brightened her spirits that day, except Storm, who'd made himself scarce again.

His actions baffled her. At times he looked at her with what she thought was admiration and maybe—just maybe— something more. This confused her, because she wasn't repulsed by it or even immune to it, but deeply affected by it.

That wasn't all. She found herself watching for him constantly and feeling crestfallen when approaching steps turned out to be someone else's. What was wrong with her? She gave it much thought as she rode, abed, on the back of the wagon.

It wasn't until bedtime that Storm finally came to see her. They'd moved her bed back to the ground near the fire, for warmth. He knelt to greet her.

"How's our popular patient?" He winked, causing Sarah's stomach to lurch. He seemed genuinely glad to see her, but if that were true, why did he seem to be avoiding her?

Automatically Sarah's hand flew to her hair, smoothing, and patting.

"Despite my growing list of admirers, I'm lonely. Can you stay and talk awhile? Aunt Emily is always with Manny at the chuck wagon, and you're always busy somewhere," she said, blushing at her boldness.

Storm smiled. "I'm a busy man, but now you have my full

attention." He made himself comfortable, sitting cross-legged on the ground beside her. "What do you want to talk about?"

"There are some things I'd like to know."

"Glad to help, if I can."

"Why are we traveling with a herd of horses?"

"Because we're returning from a cattle drive. The cattle we sold in Dodge; the horses we take back, naturally. We always bring at least three extra mounts per person. Does that answer your question?"

Sarah reclined on an elbow. "Yes, but I have another. Were you and this crew part of the noisemaking and celebrating that Saturday night in Dodge, when the cattlemen arrived?"

"Certainly not. I don't allow that kind of behavior," he said firmly and positively.

She believed him but wanted to know why.

"First of all, Indians aren't widely accepted in the Dodge City saloons—or anywhere else for that matter," he added, and a hurt look shadowed his face. He continued. "I forbid drinking anyway. I've seen too many Indians addicted to 'firewater.' We stayed, as I told you before, with my good friend Reverend Thatcher. He has a place behind the blacksmith's that he uses as a house and on Sunday as a church."

"Well, then," Sarah wanted to know, "who were those noisy men? Were they with you?"

"In a way. You see, we Indians aren't too popular with neighboring ranchers—except when it's time to take the cattle to Dodge. They invite us along and assist us, but we know they're using us to get their cattle safely to the rails.

"You see, Sarah," he explained, "the cattle trail crosses the lands of the Cherokee, Creeks, Seminoles, Chickasaw, Kiowa, and our own Comanche. The Indians on these reservations resent the ranchers driving cattle across their lands. The cattle damage and eat most of their grazing grasses. With us, they get away with paying a few pennies per head of cattle for crossing. Otherwise, the ranchers would either have to pay more or not get through at all.

"So our group was made up of four neighboring ranchers and their crews, who, by the way, will be celebrating in Dodge for another week or so."

"Don't you mind being used in this manner?" she asked.

"No, we benefit from it in other ways. The biggest brokers are waiting for us in Dodge, knowing a great number of the best cattle in the state are coming. My—*our* herd alone wouldn't draw big brokers. No sense bringing the cattle in if we can't sell them, and this way we get the best price. It also keeps us tolerated in the community." He regarded her seriously. "See what you're getting yourself into, mixing with Indians?"

She smiled wearily.

He rose. "I'll let you get some rest. Do you feel up to sitting beside Hunter tomorrow?"

"Yes, but. . . ," she looked up at him coyly. "Do you suppose I could ride a horse instead?"

"If you ride well, I can't see why not."

"Tomorrow?" Sarah could tell, from his look, something had dawned on him that would override his decision.

He frowned. "We don't have a sidesaddle."

"Oh, I never thought of that. Do I need one?" she asked hopefully.

"Sarah, the men—your skirts—"

"Couldn't I wear trousers, like you?"

His eyes twinkled with amusement. "Do you have any?"

Sarah shook her head and thought over her dilemma before exclaiming: "Could I have a pair of yours?"

He laughed. "I do have extra, but they'd be much too large."

"I'll take them! Aunt Emily is great with a needle and thread."

He shook his head, grinning. "You have a deal. I'll give your aunt the trousers and select a good mount for you. You have to ride beside me, though, or the deal's off. This is dangerous territory."

She nodded her assent, only too happy to comply.

Two days later, Sarah appeared at breakfast clad in her new pants and a white blouse. Storm helped her mount a serene-looking sorrel, which soon danced alongside Storm's large bay.

"Does my horse have a name?" she asked.

Storm grinned. "No. Does it need one?"

"Well, how am I supposed to talk to it, if I don't know its name?"

"You could name it then!" Amusement showed plainly on his face.

"Is it a girl or boy horse?"

"It's a boy."

"How about Red? He has a reddish hue, so the name fits. Like the Indians' names. By the way," she patted the horse's mane affectionately, "how did you get your name?"

"I was born during a storm. My mother named me *Thunderstorm*, but my father insisted I have a regular white man's name. Somehow, *Storm* stuck anyway. My disposition as a child must have reinforced it."

"What is your real name?"

Storm's face suddenly darkened as if a black cloud had passed over him. His forehead creased in frustrated anger.

"I prefer *Storm*. The other name is irrelevant." He quickly spurred his horse into a run.

Sarah nudged her own horse, racing after him.

Finally, Storm slowed just beyond camp. When Sarah caught up he was over his gloom and smiled his approval.

"You've passed the riding test!"

"I love riding, especially astride. My father used to let me ride like this out in the country."

"The trousers look better on you than they ever did on me!" His teasing eyes twinkled.

"Aunt Emily can do wonders with a needle and thread," she said, blushing. "By the way," Sarah looked around the

52

quiet camp, "why isn't anyone ready? The sun has been up for several minutes, and no one is prepared to leave."

"Didn't anyone tell you? Today's Sunday. We never travel on Sunday. We go to church and relax."

"Church? But where?" she asked, completely puzzled.

"Our own of course."

"But we didn't last Sunday."

"We did, you didn't. The men and I had church before you ladies were even awake. We had to hurry last week because it was vital we reached the Cimarron River in four days. Now we do it right.

"I don't usually allow working on God's appointed day of rest, but sometimes I compromise, such as when we're traveling. At the ranch, no one works on Sunday."

"No one?" she asked, hardly believing him.

He shook his head.

"Why?"

"The Book says not to, so we don't," he said simply.

"Book? What book?"

"The Holy Bible."

"Oh, that," she sighed. "I don't think you're supposed to take it quite so literally."

"I do."

"But why? No one does." She quickly added, "We're not expected to!"

He turned his horse around. "You're wrong, Sarah." Trotting off toward camp, he called over his shoulder, "C'mon, or you'll be late for church!"

Sarah couldn't believe her eyes when she saw Storm leading Indians in prayer! And the others, including Aunt Emily! The rugged men sat cross-legged on the ground around Storm as he stood, Bible in hand, leading the opening prayer. Sarah sat on a nearby log, watching in amazement. She'd thought Indians heathens!

Storm's sermon might have been for her benefit, because

..e explained the Bible's origin and why it should be respected and obeyed as the True Word of God. In all the time she'd gone to church, she'd never heard these truths. But she knew she had rarely paid attention, her mind usually on a new dress or so-and-so's stylish hat.

Storm ended his message with powerful words from his Book that backed up everything he'd preached. Surprised by Storm's knowledge of the Book, Sarah listened intently.

"It is for this reason I take the Bible literally. It's God speaking directly to me. Second Timothy 3:16 begins: 'All scripture is given by inspiration of God. . . .' He says it, and I believe it, so I live by it." Storm closed his Book and led them in a beautiful closing prayer.

Not at all like what her minister in Chicago read from a book, this prayer poured from Storm's heart as if he talked to God face to face, as if He stood right beside him—*alive* and real!

After the *amens* rang out and the men dispersed, Storm approached Sarah. How foolish she felt, having told him not an hour ago that he, a preacher, shouldn't take the Bible literally!

"I didn't know you were a preacher or so knowledgeable about the Bible," she said, trading her embarrassment for awe.

Storm smiled, caressing his Bible gently. "I learned about God and Jesus Christ from a wandering preacher lost on the way to his new church. He finally found his congregation, in Dodge City—and is, of course, my friend Andrew Thatcher.

"My father encouraged my faith by sending me to a Christian college in Kansas, where I studied theology."

"You did a fine job, preacher," she said, feeling a new type of respect for the complex, multifarious Indian-cowboy. "I enjoyed it and learned from it. Do you do this often?"

He spoke solemnly. "There's no church near the ranch, so I do the services. That's why I became a preacher. These people need God."

"You amaze me!" She chuckled, shaking her head. "And I thought you just another savage Indian!"

"I can be," he warned with a teasing smile.

His playful grin and sparkling eyes caused her knees to tremble. Her feelings were dangerously close to the surface. She quickly changed the subject.

"You owe me a ride. I rushed Aunt Emily into fixing these trousers, not knowing we don't travel on Sunday." Her blue eyes flashed at him, "Couldn't we ride just a little, so I can get used to Red?"

"That's exactly what I had in mind. In fact, I asked Manny to pack a picnic lunch. We'll leave camp for a few hours." He smiled playfully, "That is, if you trust my savage company."

With her heart pounding, she nodded. "I'm beginning to like your Book and its rules. A picnic sounds much better than another day on the trail." She smiled at him shyly, "Are you certain no one works at the ranch on Sunday?"

"That's one thing you can be sure of." Starting to walk away, he stopped to call over his shoulder, "Maybe the only thing!"

Sarah had mixed feelings about spending the day with Storm. While she trusted him completely, she worried about whether she could trust herself! She found it increasingly difficult to hide her fondness for his company. Her blood raced at the very thought of having him to herself for the whole afternoon.

But Storm appeared moments later, with Manny and Aunt Emily in tow, as well as four horses. Sarah struggled with disappointment.

After the first pangs of frustration faded, she felt relieved— perhaps she wasn't ready to be alone with Storm anyway. Besides, wasn't Aunt Emily her favorite companion? She should be delighted to have her aunt along and also have a chance to get acquainted with Manny.

Sarah welcomed the couple warmly, telling them how glad she was to have them along.

*   *   *

As they rode from camp Sarah spotted Black Feather crouched beside the chuck wagon. His venomous glare made the roots of her hair tingle with fear. Quickly she maneuvered Red alongside Storm. Though she could no longer see the spiteful Indian, she could still feel his hostile eyes. She edged her horse closer yet to Storm's.

A few miles from camp, Storm chose a meadow bordered by a dense thicket for their picnic. Bowing majestically in the breeze, bluebonnets and daisies graced their miles-long table.

A lunch eaten amid such beauty could only taste delicious. Emily and Manny had packed biscuits and honey, cheese, beef jerky, pickles, and fresh spring water. The meadow echoed with laughter and gaiety as the four enjoyed their Sunday meal.

As soon as they finished eating, Manny and Emily rushed off excitedly, in search of wild herbs for their kitchen. Storm and Sarah sat watching the rejuvenated oldsters, baskets swinging, stroll toward the nearby woods.

"Can I trust my best cook with your aunt Emily?" Storm teased.

Sarah smiled and began gathering the picnic remnants. "I can't be sure. She's changed since we've come here. This has been so good for her."

"And what about you?" Storm asked.

"I'm still adapting," Sarah whispered, eyes downcast.

Storm stood abruptly. "Do you know what I haven't done since childhood?" he asked enthusiastically. "Run through the meadow like a deer! Come Sarah," he urged, "I need you to help me keep my sanity; I believe I've caught spring fever!" Taking her hand, he pulled her along, leaping through the daisies, bluebonnets, and wildflowers. Before long Sarah became caught up in his excitement, and the two flew through the fields, hands clasped, laughing like children.

Reaching a steep hill, Storm halted abruptly. Sarah, unable to stop, tumbled to the ground. But still having Storm's hand grasped tightly, he came tumbling after! They rolled down the hill like two carefree children on a holiday.

At the bottom, they lay facing the sky, pains from laughter searing through their bodies. Panting from their exertion, the laughter simmered into less painful giggles.

Rolling onto his side, he faced Sarah and teased, "To think I fell head over heels—and over a gal with weeds in her hair and a giant daisy growing from her ear!"

"I don't!" Sarah protested, her cheeks rosy from her frolic.

"Here," Storm said leaning towards her to pluck the errant daisy. Sarah turned. Their eyes met just inches apart. Sarah knew she couldn't stop her natural inclination to meet his lips. Neither could have stopped the overpowering magnetic force.

His lips were warm from the sun and surprisingly soft for such a rugged man. For several seconds she was caught up in a whirlpool of feelings and emotions—as though slowly being sucked through a vacuum, devoid of reality. Then Sarah let all inhibitions drift with the wind. Lady or not, she clasped him around the neck and returned his kiss boldly.

Storm groaned with feeling at her response, clutching her blond tresses gently, forcing the kiss to greater depths.

Yet it was he who reluctantly pulled away, Sarah knew, because the feeling of a wonderful moment lost was too vivid to forget.

The warm breeze cooled her lips, still damp from the kiss. Storm stood, pulling her with him.

Sarah's first impulse was to hide her look of love from him; then she banished the thought. Why hide the most honest, wholesome emotion she'd ever felt?

Staring intently into her eyes, Storm finally groaned, ran his fingers through his hair, and whispered, "Sarah, you could make me forget all my responsibilities."

"We could share them. . . ."

He rubbed her hands gently between his. "It's time for a long talk, Sarah." Leading her to a fallen tree, he motioned her to sit, while he stood leaning on his knee, his leg propped casually on the log.

"I brought you here today for a reason. I've put off telling you a few things that cannot be postponed any longer."

Sarah gave him a puzzled look.

He sighed. "Sarah, my legal name is Wilson Clarke. Your grandfather and my father are one and the same," he said quickly, lest he hesitate and lose his courage.

Speechless, Sarah could only stare up at him, her mouth slightly agape.

With calm voice and steady gaze he said, "You realize I couldn't tell you before. The way you felt about Indians. . . . Then I just didn't know how to begin. Now, of course—I have to tell you—uncles don't go around kissing their nieces! Sarah, I'm sorry. I should never have let it happen."

Gazing into his earnest, smoky eyes, Sarah's emotions windmilled. How she loved this man! Nothing he said lessened that. Nor was she sorry or ashamed of her emotion. She stubbornly refused to give up what she'd so recently discovered.

Sarah dropped her intent gaze and bluntly proclaimed, "It's too late. I love you."

With impatience and frustration, he ran his fingers through his dark hair and rolled his eyes heavenward.

"Sarah—"

"No, let me finish," she quieted him. "I may never again have the courage to say this. You're only a half uncle. I know my emotions and my heart. Even if my love isn't returned, I can't change the way I feel."

"Sarah, there's more. Please listen."

She obeyed his firm command.

He hesitated, measuring her carefully. *"You're my enemy,* Sarah," he enunciated in an impatient yet gentle tone. "My father left Arrow C to *me!* Born and bred there, I've run it for three years. It's mine, and I'll prove it when I find the other will. I know it exists, because my father told me about it before he died. Yet after his death the only will found was the old one, made out before I was born, stating the ranch should go to his son, your father, or to his children. But that changed! *He left the ranch to me!*" he stated emphatically.

Sarah didn't care about owning the ranch and started to tell him so, but he silenced her.

"There's more." He sat beside her on the log, taking her hands in his. "I'm betrothed." His eyes dropped, unable to meet hers.

Sarah studied him intently. "How can you marry a girl you don't love?"

Storm frowned. "What makes you think I don't?"

"The mutual response to that kiss," she flared.

"That kiss was a mistake and shouldn't have happened. Little Bird is a wonderful, beautiful Indian girl. But how I feel about her doesn't matter. I gave her *my word*—before I met you.

"We would have been married by now, but I refused to make the commitment until the ranch was legally mine. What do I have to offer a wife? I'm just a trail boss and ranch manager—" he spoke gently, yet firmly. "Besides that's being a step down for me, I find it frustrating working for a woman who has never seen a ranch in her life!"

Sarah held her tongue, knowing how easily she could say something she'd regret. Storm had stepped completely out of character. It almost seemed as if he were baiting her, urging an argument.

While confused and still digesting all she'd heard, one thing she knew for sure. She'd not give up the ranch so he could marry a woman he didn't love. Never.

Studying him, Sarah could almost see his inner battle for control. Beads of sweat made a mustache on his smooth upper lip, and she longed to kiss his throbbing temple.

"Don't you ever get angry?" she asked. "With all the deep

feelings you've been harboring, why aren't you raving? Why did you offer to escort 'your enemy' to the ranch? Surely you don't want me there. I'd never have guessed you considered me an enemy. Why have you been so kind to me?"

"Because," he explained, "the Bible says we should love and pray for our enemies. The Book also tells me to lay my burden at His feet and He will take it. I've done this. The problem is no longer mine, it's His. I trust Him to work it out the way He sees fit."

She shook her head in disbelief, "I don't understand. I'm your enemy, yet you feel no antagonism toward me? Don't you realize that by giving up the Indian girl for me, you'd also acquire the ranch you want so much?"

Storm's square jaw tightened.

"I wouldn't accept the ranch *that* way! What kind of man do you think I am?" His eyes flashed like flaming steel.

"Ah," said Sarah smiling, "finally. Is that anger I detect?"

"Yes, I'm angry," his voice rose and his eyes flashed dangerously. "I am, after all, human."

Sarah stopped grinning and nodded toward the two figures slowly approaching. With hands on hips, she spoke sternly.

"Let me say one thing before Aunt Emily and Manny get here, Storm. Your rejection of me doesn't change how I feel. I love you, and that's why I'm so angry. Love makes me care what happens to you. If you marry someone you don't love, for whatever reason, you're not only cheating her, but yourself as well.

"I may love you, Storm, but until you call off this . . . this ridiculous wedding, I . . . I . . . I hate you!" she spat tearfully. She turned and ran toward Emily and Manny, leaving Storm frozen by her words.

~ 5 ~

When they broke camp the next morning, Storm didn't bring Sarah's horse as she'd hoped, so she climbed up beside Hunter, with Aunt Emily.

Between the hot weather and Sarah's soreness from yesterday's riding, she squirmed uncomfortably. Aunt Emily smiled knowingly and suggested they walk a while. Sarah welcomed the idea—although she had to promise Hunter she'd stay near the wagon and not pick up sticks!

Glancing upward as she walked, Sarah marveled at the blueness of the sky. Not one cloud obscured her view of the deep heavens. How she wished her life were like that Oklahoma sky! Feeling shaded by the darkness of her own private, hovering cloud, she wondered if confiding in her aunt would lift her spirits.

"Aunt Emily, is it acceptable for a woman to tell a man how she feels about him?" Sarah finally asked.

"She can certainly let him know she finds him interesting," Emily said thoughtfully. "A little encouragement can't hurt. After all this is 1876! Things have changed since—" she broke off abruptly, pointing toward the brush. "Look, a rabbit!"

Sarah turned in time to see a brown hare dodge the wagon's wheels and scurry into the sparse brush.

"It reminds me of how I must have looked to Storm when we first met," Sarah sighed sadly, "like a frightened, cornered rabbit."

"Uh-oh! That sigh means you have a problem. Best get it off your chest and into the air. Let's have it," her aunt urged.

Sarah poured out the story of yesterday's adventure with Storm, with the exception of the kiss. That belonged to them. To tell about that would somehow soil the memory.

Keeping silent until Sarah finished, Emily then clucked, "Sarah, Sarah, Sarah." She shook her head, frowning. "A relationship with Storm is out of the question, if he's kin. Surely you cannot be in love with your own uncle—your father's half brother! Do you realize what you're saying?" Aunt Emily's face mirrored her disgust.

"Cousins marry, and surely we aren't even that close, because he isn't a real uncle—only my father's *half* brother," Sarah argued.

"I don't know, Sarah. I don't like it. And to tell him of your love so boldly, oh, Sarah—"

"But it's true," Sarah admitted with feeling. "You know how I hate pretense."

"I also recall the trouble your bold remarks caused when you were younger." Emily's face and voice softened. "I'll never forget the time you asked Mrs. DeWitt if she truly had a skeleton in her closet! We had to be mighty careful what we said around you!" Aunt Emily laughed softly. "Reverend Hammond regrets the day he asked how you liked his sermon. Remember, you told him loudly that it was the boringest sermon you'd ever heard and that you were never coming to church again."

"Aunt Emily, I was only four!"

"You may have toned down your frankness a mite since then."

"I see nothing wrong with being honest," Sarah declared.

Emily sighed, "Well, at least it's leap year. You know what they say: 'Leap year is a time when women can be bolder than usual.' "

Sarah scuffed along beside her aunt. "I don't regret telling him that I love him; it's the truth, and I have nothing to hide." She held her head high with pride.

"Have you heard about someone at the ranch called Little Bird?" Sarah asked.

"No, and don't ask me to question Manny." Aunt Emily gave her a sideways look. "I hate that sort of thing, and you know it."

Sarah pursed her lips. "I won't. I'll find out somehow."

"Of course, if the subject comes up. . . ."

Sarah smiled lovingly. "I do love him, Aunt Emily," she said, smiling tearfully. "Please try to understand."

Emily stopped to fold her niece into her arms. "If it will make you feel better, I can tell you one thing. He worried plenty when that snake bit you! I never saw a man fret so! That enemy business doesn't make sense. Had you died from that snakebite, he'd have had the ranch. Yet he did everything he could to help you recover, including constant prayer. I heard him. And at one point. . . ," she hesitated, as if unsure if she should relate the rest.

"At one point, what?" pressed Sarah anxiously.

"I don't feel right telling—"

"Aunt Emily! Tell me what you started to say. At one point, what?"

"Well, at one point I saw him pleading with God, and his eyes got sorta misty. I think he cares more than he realizes."

"Or," Sarah added, "he promised to deliver me safely to Mr. Lewis and worried he'd be blamed if something dreadful happened to me!"

"You don't really believe that, Sarah!"

Sarah kicked a pebble, sending it cavorting into the air, to plop down in the dust several feet ahead. "No. I don't. His eyes soften when he looks at me. Instinct tells me he cares, but he's extremely disciplined.

"Aunt Emily, I just have to make him see *he can't marry Little Bird.*"

After supper that evening, sitting upon the wagon bed, Sarah conversed with her Indian friends and Leo, Manny, and Emily. Storm sat alone by the fire, reading his Book.

Sarah, thinking about her dilemma, was suddenly struck by an idea. "Will you take me for a walk, Snakebite?"

He nodded, his smile showing pride at being asked.

As they strolled around the circle of the wagons Sarah asked insignificant questions about the ranch, then blurted quickly: "Tell me about Little Bird. What is she like?"

"Little Bird?" he repeated. "She is pretty, like you."

"Thank you, Snakebite. But what is she like on the inside?" Sarah prodded.

"She changes like the seasons. Has many faces."

"What do you mean, Snakebite?"

"I mean, she is nice one day, the next day not nice. She is nice in front of some, not so nice front of others. She picks a face that fits, like an Indian picks a name that fits," he explained thoughtfully.

"What face does she wear for Storm?"

"Always she wears her best face for Storm. He never sees the other faces. Others try to tell Storm, but he does not listen."

Sarah was now more determined than ever to stop Storm from marrying the Indian girl.

Sarah thought they would never reach their destination, for it seemed as if she'd been traveling her whole life. She could barely recall a time when she hadn't been moving. It was now more than six weeks since leaving Chicago.

* * *

Several mornings after the picnic, Storm brought Sarah her horse, with an invitation to ride with him. Not having spoken more than two words to him since, she swallowed her pride and accepted his offer. Her desire to ride overwhelmed her desire to stay angry.

After riding hours without conversation, they were startled by their first encounter with other travelers. They had just crested a hill, Storm a bit ahead of Sarah, when he stopped abruptly and reached back for her hand, which he held protectively.

"Now, don't panic," he warned calmly. "We have company, but there's nothing to fear."

Sarah peeked around him and saw a large group of people slowly approaching on foot. Her blood raced slightly when she recognized them as Indians. Storm's presence and her recent experiences with the crew enabled her to watch their approach without trembling.

She counted twenty men, ten women, and numerous children, including infants strapped tightly to their mothers' backs. Some nodded in passing, while others stared curiously at the blond lady and the handsome half-breed.

The men had cropped hair and wore multicolored shirts and plain trousers. The women's dress appeared less colorful, and some wore blankets on their shoulders against the morning chill.

One pleasant-faced young man stopped and addressed Storm in a language Sarah didn't recognize. Storm answered with a few Indian words, accompanied by sign language, which the young Indian promptly returned.

When the Indians had passed, Storm explained that they were near the Arapaho Indian reservation and that she shouldn't be alarmed or frightened upon meeting more. Often he stopped to point out small groups of teepees and crude huts, arranged to form small villages within the appropriated government land.

The following day they met a group of Apache and later a

group of Kiowa and Comanche whom Storm knew from Fort Sill, which lay a few miles east of their trail.

As they neared Texas the dawns lost their coldness, becoming just crisp and invigorating. One morning Storm allowed the ladies to bathe in a small creek branching from the great Red River. He kept the men, who had bathed earlier, at the wagons, while Emily and Sarah enjoyed their rare treat.

With the Wichita Mountains steepling to one side and a group of fragrant pines fencing in the other, Sarah donned her pants again, hoping that Storm would invite her to ride. She knew this might be her last chance to talk to him before reaching the ranch, for Storm had announced that if all went well they would reach the Red River crossing by late afternoon and the ranch by nightfall. She'd given much thought to their situation and had a proposal to offer him.

Still pink from scrubbing, the ladies approached the crew. Sarah flashed Storm a smile of delight as he held out Red's reins. Lifting her high into the air, he set Sarah upon the horse as though she were a mere child.

Storm gave the men instructions before galloping far ahead with Sarah. Once the others were out of sight, they slowed to an even trot, side by side. But neither spoke.

Sarah finally broke the strained silence. "Thank you for letting me ride."

He spoke flatly without looking at her. "The weather's been good, and we've made excellent time, so I can't see any reason why you shouldn't."

They rode in silence again, until Sarah's impatience wore thin. "Storm," she blurted, edging close, touching his arm, "look me in the eyes and tell me you're in love with Little Bird."

He stopped his horse, but didn't look at her. "I told you,

Sarah, I have no choice. I gave my word. Love has nothing to do with it."

"Please look at me, Storm!" she pleaded. "Listen, I'll prove that my concern is with *your* welfare and not mine." Sarah took a deep breath, then quickly blurted, "If you promise not to marry Little Bird, I'll sign the ranch over to you now and return to Chicago."

Sarah hesitated, returning the intense glare of stunned gray eyes. "I mean it. You need never see me again, but you'll be free to marry someone you love. You're a wonderful man and deserve happiness."

Sarah's heart lurched as Storm blinked his eyes.

"You'd do that?" he whispered huskily.

"I would. Just say the word."

He squinted as if his answer caused pain. "I can't." He looked upward and said, as if memorized: "I'm committed to Little Bird. I gave my word."

"Suit yourself then," Sarah snapped in reckless anger. "Then I'll fight for the ranch! My name is on the will! I'm Wilson's legal granddaughter, and even if there is a second will—which I doubt—I'll contest it. You'd have to prove you're Wilson's son, and unless your parents were legally married—which I also doubt—you can't inherit. I'll do everything I can to keep you from getting the ranch and marrying Little Bird," she flared, then dug her heels into Red.

Angry and frustrated, Sarah urged Red on until the scenery sped by so quickly that her vision became reduced to a multicolored blur. Riding with her face flat against Red's mane, she heard Storm's frantic calling but only pressed Red harder.

Suddenly, her saddle snapped from Red's girth. She clung to it with feet still in the stirrups and her hands still clutching the reins. She was being dragged along the dusty trail by her feet. Storm's horse pounded fiercely behind her.

Then she lost hold of the stirrups. Her clasp on the reins

had become her only connection with the horse; she tightened her hold.

"Sarah, no! Let go! Drop the reins!" Storm yelled.

She obeyed, rolling over and over before landing on her back as Red thundered off, saddle dragging in the dust.

Sliding off his horse, Storm ran to Sarah's side.

He cradled her head. "Are you all right?"

She gasped. "I-I'm . . . alive, anyway!"

"Do you hurt anywhere?" he asked frantically.

She gulped, "Yes, everywhere!"

Hugging her head to his chest, he kissed her forehead gently.

Sarah ached from head to toe, but in Storm's strong arms she felt the familiar magnetism. Gazing up into worried gray eyes, her mouth trembled with anticipation. His lips touched hers softly, tenderly, lingering sweetly until tears slipped from Sarah's eyes. Filled to capacity with love, her tears overflowed.

Storm ended the kiss, not abruptly, but reluctantly. He gathered her into his arms, his cheek against hers, until tears dampened his face, alarming him.

"You *are* hurt! You're crying! Sarah, where do you hurt? Your legs?" he began checking them for breaks.

"I'm all right." She wiped the tears with the back of her hand. "Where's Red?"

He helped her stand, insisting she walk and move every moveable part. Only when she passed this test did he mount his horse and reluctantly ride off in search of Red.

Alone, Sarah wondered how she could have fallen so helplessly in love. And what linked Little Bird and Storm, keeping him stubbornly bound to the Indian girl? It wasn't love. What was it? Sarah sensed Storm's reluctance to marry the girl, yet he refused to call it off. Why had he made such a binding vow?

When Storm returned with Red in tow, Sarah noticed

immediately that something had upset him. He'd been in such a tender mood—what could have disturbed him?

"What is it?" she asked as he dismounted.

He paused, measuring her carefully. "Your saddle strap was cut."

"Cut?" she exclaimed. "By whom?"

Stroking Red's mane, he frowned, not looking at her.

"You know who did it, don't you?" she accused.

"I think so."

"Who?"

"Black Feather offered to saddle the horses—" Storm began.

"Black Feather!" She recalled his hostile looks and cold attempts at friendship. "Why would he want me hurt?"

"It had to be an accident. Perhaps the saddle was cut by thorns, or—"

"Isn't Black Feather Little Bird's brother?" she demanded.

He nodded. "I'm sorry this happened and relieved you weren't hurt. I'll investigate the matter thoroughly before I accuse anyone."

Storm scooped Sarah up and placed her gently upon his horse and climbed up behind her.

"For now we'll have to ride double." He reached around her for the reins.

"Cozy, isn't it?" teased Sarah, twisting around to look at him.

"Behave, Sarah!" He laughed, but beneath his jovial tone, Sarah detected stiff tenseness. "You're making things difficult for me, you know?"

"I know," she said smugly, settling her small back against his hard, broad chest.

Gently, Storm placed her away from him but then unintentionally urged the horse forward too suddenly, and Sarah fell back against him, where she seemed to fit so perfectly and naturally. He shrugged and rode on.

*   *   *

That afternoon they reached the Red River and safely crossed into Texas, where they camped for refreshment.

Manny and Emily served the remainder of the beef jerky and cheese. They hungrily ate the remains of yesterday's corn, bartered from a reservation Kiowa. Laughter rippled through the group, who were glad to be near home.

Sarah searched the gathering for Storm but found him missing. Black Feather was also absent. Could Storm be questioning him?

Had Black Feather cut her saddle strap? Who wanted her harmed? Did someone want her frightened away? *Or*, she shivered as she thought, *dead?*

Edging her way to the horse corral, Sarah spied Black Feather rubbing down a horse, but Storm was not in sight. She backed away quickly, not wanting to be seen by Black Feather.

She took the long way back, skirting the wagons, edging near the woods but stopped abruptly upon hearing a man speaking. Recognizing Storm's voice, she followed it silently. Just into the woods she spied him kneeling beside a fallen log, pleading fervently. But with whom? He appeared to be alone. She listened.

". . . You've worked miracles in my life before, Lord. I need Your help, again. Your Book says 'Cast thy burden upon the Lord, and he shall sustain thee.' Here's my burden, Father. Sustain me. Give me the strength and knowledge to do Thy will. Amen."

Storm sat with head bowed after ending his prayer, giving Sarah time to scurry back to the others, but his prayer stuck with her. How she wished she could pray like that—to have a loving friend to guide her, as he did! She made up her mind to ask him how she could get on similar terms with God.

The sun was just setting when they reached the approach to the ranch. A large wooden sign arched over the gravel road, anchored on either side by large, weathered posts. A giant arrow, bent to form the letter C, dominated the sign, and carved letters spelled out *Arrow C Ranch* beneath.

Sarah rode beside Storm as they passed under the entrance.

"Welcome to your new home."

"Do you mean that?" she asked.

"When I find the will, you'll be welcome as long as you wish to stay."

"Thank you. And may I extend the same courtesy to you? As long as the ranch is mine, you're not only welcome, but needed. I don't know the first thing about running a ranch."

"May the Lord find an answer for us both," he said.

As a plain structure came into view, he asked, "Well, what do you think?"

Sarah's enthusiasm faded. It seemed small compared to what she had been used to in Chicago. Wooden and only one floor, it appeared bleak and unwelcoming. Her disappointment showed, and Storm let out his stifled laugh.

"Sarah, that's the bunkhouse!" He sobered and pointed beyond, to his far right. "There on the hill stands the house."

"Oh-h, it's beautiful!" Sarah sighed, noting the proud look her remark brought.

The sun, slowly sinking behind the large gray-and-white house, framed it in blazing red. The fieldstone structure, graced by a full-length front porch supported by six square posts, stood proudly on the hill and seemed to beckon her warmly. She felt welcomed by the house, as if she'd come home after a long absence.

People poured out of the house and adjacent barn. A large Mexican hurried out to take their horses.

"Thanks, Joseph, how is everything?" Storm greeted.

"*Si*, everything good, *señor*," he replied jovially.

Storm introduced Sarah to many new faces in the next few moments, but only two immediately impressed her. Storm's mother, a lovely, bronzed, middle-aged Indian woman received Sarah with curious eyes but definite aloofness.

The next introduction sent Sarah's hand flying to Storm's arm for support. Almost reluctantly, he introduced Little Bird, whose lovely, dimpled cheeks smiled up at Storm in obvious admiration. But that wasn't what alarmed Sarah. Little Bird's swollen form caused Sarah to lose her balance. The lovely Indian girl stood proudly, heavy with child.

~ 6 ~

*A*s if embarrassed by Little Bird's condition, Storm hurriedly excused himself, leaving Sarah and Aunt Emily in his mother's care. Dawn motioned them toward the house.

Storm's mother dressed not in buckskin or a blanket, as Sarah had envisioned, but a loose, flowing, yellow dress. She looked as much the lady as—Sarah looked down at her own dusty blouse and Storm's remodeled pants—certainly *more* the lady than she!

As Dawn led them through the front door Sarah marveled at her gracefulness. She appeared almost regal, with her hair parted in the center and long braids wound around her head to form a crown. Her prominent forehead and high cheekbones were held proudly, while only slight mouth and eye creases marked her as old enough to be Storm's mother.

Little Bird's eyes narrowed as they followed Sarah into the house. Sarah would have recognized her as Black Feather's sister, if only by her unwelcome stare.

They entered into a spacious living room with a two-story-high beamed ceiling. A curved staircase wound up to the second floor, where every door was visible over a white

73

latticed balcony framing the length of the hall. Sarah was pleased to find the house not only lovely, but clean, tastefully furnished, and cool.

The floor plan suited Sarah. The four bedroom doors stood in full view of the living room, giving her a comforting sense of security.

Dawn spoke slowly but with perfect diction. "I'll show you and Miss Ruggles to your rooms." Her tone, however, showed no sign of warmth.

A stout, robust-looking Mexican woman burst into the room.

"Here's Rosa," Dawn announced. She introduced the house cook to the ladies, stiffly.

Rosa smiled amicably, fairly bursting with excitement.

Sarah liked Rosa immediately. Her greeting offered friendship and hospitality, something not yet offered by anyone else at Arrow C.

"Welcome, welcome. Ah," Rosa inspected Sarah from head to toe, "it will be pleasure to work for so pretty a young lady. *Si.*"

Rosa also extended a friendly welcome to Aunt Emily before turning back to her kitchen. Before disappearing through the large swinging door, she called over her shoulder, "I make special supper, *si.* One hour."

A large four-poster dominated the master bedroom, the last door along the open upstairs hallway. The room and its furnishings were decorated with a definitely masculine touch. A brown quilt covered the bed, which stood between two floor-to-ceiling windows, draped in gold velvet pulled back to let in the light. The colors complemented the brown-hued carpet and walnut furniture.

On the other side of the room stood two gold brocade Queen Anne chairs, placed at a tête-à-tête angle.

Sarah's puzzlement at the decor prompted Dawn's explanation.

"This was Wilson's room. I thought it should now be yours."

Sarah glanced about the room slowly. The thought of staying in her grandfather's room pleased her and gave her a feeling of closeness to the man she'd never met.

"But where is your room?" Sarah asked, wondering why her grandfather's wife wasn't staying in the room they must have shared so recently.

Dawn remained cool but polite. "When Wilson became ill, I moved into the smaller room next to this one." She nodded to the small adjoining door. "But it's your home now. You tell me where to sleep." Dawn stood tall and met Sarah's eyes head-on. "I wanted to leave, but Storm insisted I stay. I hope you don't mind. I'll work, of course, to earn my keep. I do most of the cleaning."

Sarah studied the proud woman and chose her words carefully. "I have no wish to disrupt the home you've known for so long, and I wouldn't think of your leaving. I'll need you to teach me the workings of a rancher's home. As for the cleaning, I hope you'll let me help."

Sarah hesitated. "Where does Storm sleep?"

Dawn searched Sarah's face intently. "Storm sleeps in the bunkhouse usually, although sometimes I find him on the couch in the study after a long night working on the books."

Dawn bit her lip before blurting, "Are you sure you wouldn't rather have your aunt in the adjoining room?"

When Sarah shook her head, Dawn turned toward the door. "You had better rest. I'll have water and towels sent up so you can wash. Don't forget supper is in one hour."

Sarah had to admire Dawn's graciousness, if not her warmth. What did she expect? She was the enemy—to these people anyway.

Sarah's mind didn't dwell on Dawn or her lack of hospitality, but skipped to Little Bird and her condition. So *that* was Storm's responsibility! How could she fight it? She couldn't. Breaking up a loveless relationship was one thing, splitting a family another!

Wearily, she sank into the armchair. What could she do? There was only one solution. She'd give Storm the ranch so he could marry Little Bird, and she'd return to Chicago before she got too fond of the place. Tears streamed down her cheeks, but she didn't bother to wipe them away. What was the use? New ones would only replace them.

The memory of Storm's prayer jarred her from self-pity. Should she try talking to God? She'd never prayed with her own words, for her family had specific prayers for every occasion. Storm had made talking to God seem easy and natural. How she needed a friend like that!

Slipping to her knees as she'd seen Storm do in the woods, she folded her hands and looked upward. "Dear God. You know me, though I don't know You. I'd like to change that. Storm doesn't worry about things, for he claims You'll take care of everything. Will You do that for me, too? Knowing my feelings for Storm, will You help? Can I leave this burden with You as Storm left his burden?

"I know our relationship is not like Yours and Storm's, but maybe You could show me how I can know You better. I haven't lived according to the Bible, like Storm, but I intend to learn. Thank You, Amen."

Her own words echoed back: "I haven't lived according to the Bible, like Storm." That was her answer! Storm lives the Bible! He couldn't be responsible for Little Bird's condition! Her discovery pleased her. Something else linked Storm to Little Bird.

"Thank You, God," she whispered. "You've helped me already. How could I have thought, even for a moment, that Your friend Storm could possibly. . . ."

Yet, she pondered, something *linked Storm to Little Bird. But what?*

A light knock sounded. Sarah looked up to see Aunt Emily tiptoeing in like a naughty child.

"It's only me. What are you doing on the floor? Did you lose something?"

"No, Aunt Emily, I'm praying—like Storm!"

"I knew he'd be a good influence on you." She sat down on the bed. "Which is why I sneaked in as soon as I could. When I saw Little Bird's condition, I knew the time had come to question Manny."

"Storm would never—" Sarah faltered, at a loss for words.

"You're right, it wasn't Storm," her aunt stated matter-of-factly.

Sarah's bewildered look prompted Emily to confess: "His father, which is why he feels responsible."

"My grandfather? But I thought he and Dawn . . . ?"

"Manny said Wilson Clarke's marriage to Dawn was a Comanche ceremony, recognized by Indians only. Manny claims Wilson seemed a virtuous man, but it appears he turned out to be quite a scoundrel. Dawn herself admits her husband's probable guilt."

"I see. So that's how it was. Grandfather could be the baby's father. He's only been dead six months." Sarah put her hands to her cheeks and exclaimed, "Poor Storm!"

The wet grass darkened the tips of Sarah's walking shoes. Rising early, dressed in Storm's remodeled pants, Sarah made her way to the stable for Red. Before entering the barn, she gazed back at the ranch in the morning sunlight.

Thick, green lawns framed the three largest structures: the ranch house, the stable, and the bunkhouse. Beside the bunkhouse stood a small barn, and Sarah could see several other small buildings scattered randomly about the ranch. Several beautiful trees graced Arrow C, and Sarah recognized the white oak, bald cypress, mesquite, and southern magnolia. She selected the large cottonwood in back for afternoon reading; its thick branches would supply good, cool shade.

This morning, from her bedroom window, she had spied a stream running behind the house, and she was anxious to explore.

She quietly entered the stable. Except for a dozen or so horses, it looked empty. Spotting Red, Sarah greeted him with a pat on the nose. Could she saddle him herself? She'd better learn, if she was to be mistress of the ranch.

Grabbing a saddle she found hanging over the stall divider, she tried to swing it over the horse's back as she'd seen the crew do numerous times. But the heavy saddle slipped from her grasp, plunging to the ground with a loud thump.

Next thing she knew, Broken Wing's head appeared over the side of another stall, and he had his rifle aimed at her with his good arm.

"Broken Wing!" she gasped.

"I almost shoot you for horse thief!"

"Were you sleeping here?"

"I always sleep with horses."

"Sorry I startled you," she apologized. "I want to ride, but can't quite manage saddling my horse."

"Broken Wing show." He stood his rifle against the wall. His useless arm swung heavily at his side as he walked around the stall.

"I teach you to care for horse good."

Sarah noticed that while Broken Wing seldom smiled, his warm friendliness was easily perceived through his gentle kindness.

With Red saddled and her first lesson on horse care over, Sarah loped toward the fields behind the house.

She delighted in the crooked, shallow stream of rapidly flowing water bubbling over smooth, shiny rocks. Seeing a wooden bridge crossing the brook, she dismounted, tying Red to a bush nearby.

Stopping midway across the bridge, she leaned over the

smooth, well-worn railing. How lovely! In the distance she saw the back of the ranch and nearby a field of bluebonnets and daisies. The meadow reminded her of the one she and Storm had romped through in Oklahoma.

She closed her eyes. How peaceful! The only sound was the gurgling of shallow water rushing over rocks. This would be her spot, where she would come to be alone with God and nature.

Daydreaming, Sarah thought about last night, her first at the ranch, and the wonderful dinner Rosa had cooked—especially appreciated after the simple meals on the trail. Storm, quiet and curiously glum, had been there, of course. Dawn, still cool but cordial, had continued to scrutinize Sarah closely. Little Bird had remained silent and sullen, her regular duties as assisting housekeeper relieved, due to her condition.

Approaching hoofbeats broke into the morning stillness and Sarah's thoughts. Her heart pounded in recognition. Storm!

He dismounted and joined her on the little bridge. "So you've found my secret place!"

"No," she blurted, "*my* secret place!"

His eyes narrowed and his jaw tightened. "Sorry, I forgot. *Your* place."

"Oh, Storm! When I said *my*, I didn't mean 'own.' Anyone can have a special place without actually owning it. Honestly, I didn't mean it the way you think."

Ignoring her apology, he leaned against the rail and looked out over the brook. Sarah watched him loosen and relax as he gazed over the lovely scenery as she had moments earlier.

"*Our* place is lovely," Sarah whispered.

Still he said nothing.

"Storm," she touched his arm lightly, "why didn't you mention Little Bird's condition?"

He frowned. "I had thought of it. But how does one tell a

properly bred young Chicago woman that her deceased grandfather is to become a father? To say nothing of the fact that the mother is not his wife and an Indian to boot.'' He shook his head. ''Things are so messed up; you'll never understand how this all happened.''

''When I first saw Little Bird,'' Sarah said shyly, ''I thought. . . . I thought. . . .''

''I know what you thought. You nearly fainted.'' He stared ahead at the swift-running water.

''But before anyone told me, I knew it wasn't true. Know how I knew?'' she asked, smiling up at him. ''I talked to God, just like you do, and before the prayer was over, He'd already given me an answer. I knew you lived from His Book and could never dishonor anyone.''

''Thank you, Sarah,'' he said. ''Now do you understand why I'm committed to Little Bird?''

''I understand why you think you are. *We* can provide for Little Bird and her baby. You don't *have* to marry her.''

''I gave her my word.''

''Couldn't you explain? Tell her about us?'' Sarah pleaded. ''If she knew you were in love with another, would she still want to marry you?''

Storm turned and looked at her for the first time since joining her on the bridge. ''What makes you think I'm in love with another?'' His face remained serious, yet his eyes teased.

''If you aren't, your kisses lie, and so do your eyes!''

''But you're my enemy, remember?''

She looked up at him in puzzlement. ''Why have you treated me so kindly, if I'm such a threat to you?''

''I told you before, the Bible says to love our enemies, but perhaps I carried that too far.'' He walked slowly toward the homeward side of the bridge.

''Storm,'' Sarah called, following him. ''Will God be my friend, too? Will He listen to me even though I've never thought much about Him before?''

"The Bible says *all* who come will be received." He turned and placed his hands on her shoulders. "But there is something you can do to assure yourself that you belong to Him." At her puzzled look he beckoned, "Come, sit under this tree with me for a moment."

When she obeyed, he took her hand. "Do you believe the Bible is the True Word of God?"

She nodded.

"Then you'll want to obey God?"

"Yes."

"It says in the Book of John, if a person wants to see the Kingdom of God, he must be born again. Now you've already been born once; we all have. God wants a second birth for us. He wants us to be born of His Spirit. In other words, let God's Spirit dwell here," he thumped on his chest, "within your heart."

"How can I do that?"

"He's always willing to enter but must be invited."

"And when I invite His Spirit, I'll be His?"

"If you're sincere, yes."

Sarah stood and walked purposefully toward her horse.

"Where are you going?" he asked.

"To my room. I'm going to invite the Spirit in right now. God and I have a lot of catching up to do!" As her horse galloped away, she waved and shouted over her shoulder, "Thanks, preacher!"

While Sarah dressed for dinner, Dawn paid her a visit.

"My son asked me to give you this." She held out a small Bible.

"Storm?" Her eyes sparkled as she hugged the Book.

Dawn watched her carefully before whispering, "You love Storm, don't you?"

Apprehensively, Sarah nodded. "Does that anger you?" she asked softly.

Dawn smiled at her for the first time. "It pleases me."

"But I thought you didn't like me. I own the ranch that should belong to your son."

"Come, sit down," she urged Sarah. They settled into the two Queen Anne chairs. "Storm and I had a talk last night. He told me everything. What touched me most was your offer to give him the ranch and go back to Chicago if he gave up Little Bird. Only in love could you do that. Anyone who loves my son that much has me for a slave."

"No, Dawn," Sarah corrected, "a friend."

Dawn rose and embraced Sarah. "Storm is wrong to marry Little Bird. We must stop him."

"But how? I've tried everything." Sarah pouted.

Dawn patted Sarah's arm. "We'll find the other will!"

Sarah bit her lip. "*Is* there another will?"

"Yes!" Dawn exclaimed. "Wilson and I decided on it long before he died. Wilson claimed he'd drawn up another will with his lawyer, but it couldn't have been Mr. Lewis, for Lewis vows Wilson never mentioned a second will. Storm says Wilson actually showed it to him once. We must find it!"

"But what good will that do?" asked Sarah. "Then he'll marry Little Bird, and I'll be on my way to Chicago."

"We'll find it, but not for him, for us. We'll hide or destroy it so Storm will never find it," Dawn said. "It's in this house somewhere."

Sarah jumped up excitedly. "We'll start today! One of us will begin at the top of the house, the other at the bottom."

"Good." Dawn smiled warmly at Sarah. "I'll take the bottom."

The attic surprised Sarah by being clean and recently dusted, which probably meant it had already been searched. But having given Dawn her word, she began her quest for the will the very next afternoon.

Full of broken furniture, worn mattresses, and old trunks, the attic felt hot and stuffy, but Sarah searched every piece of furniture, fingered every mattress lump, and rummaged through all the clothing in every trunk.

The clothes, she noted, must have been her grand-mother's—they were of that era. They intrigued her. In a spotted mirror atop an old dresser, she held dress after dress up to herself, posing prettily for each.

As she picked up a blue silk, something rolled out of the bodice, thumping to the floor. Sarah stooped to retrieve it. Just an old book! She cast it aside. Modeling dresses until the light began to fade, she decided to conclude her search for the day. Prepared to leave, she spotted the old book, shrugged, then pocketed it. One never knew when a good book might come in handy.

Over the dinner table Dawn and Sarah shared secret looks, for they were conspirators. They had something else in common—they both loved Storm and plotted against him for his own good.

Sarah wondered if it was God's Spirit within her that changed her outlook. Despite her problems, she felt happy and often found herself humming and whistling. She found herself full of love for everyone, including Little Bird.

Sarah smiled often at Little Bird, offering to do things for her, but no matter how well-meaning Sarah's gestures were, they only served to further infuriate the Indian girl.

After Sarah had been at the ranch a week, Storm announced it was high time she made an inspection of her ranch.

"The crew is disappointed that you haven't come to inspect their work. For days they've been excited and buzzing like bees, seeing that everything is perfect."

"I had no idea. Why didn't you tell me?" Sarah asked.

He smiled lazily, "I just did."

Later, on horseback, Sarah and Storm approached the far side of the stable, where a large fenced area was attached to the barn. Broken Wing greeted them with a wave. "I breaking Black; you watch?"

After dismounting, Storm plucked Sarah from her horse and placed her on the fencepost. Standing close beside her, he rested his elbows on the fence.

From the barn, Broken Wing led out a frisky, oversized, ebony stallion. The horse's shiny skin rippled with excitement as it pranced in place, scuffing the ground and whinnying furiously with wide, flaring nostrils.

"Oh, Storm, he's not going to try riding him, is he?"

"Not yet. Watch."

Broken Wing walked the horse around the pen several times, talking softly. When he tried to stroke Black's mane, the horse shook convulsively, bucking and snorting wildly at his touch.

They sat for almost an hour, watching Broken Wing's advances being thwarted by Black before he finally tolerated the Indian's gentle touch.

"Broken Wing, I'm impressed," praised Sarah.

Broken Wing smiled with pride. "Riding him next step. Will try in few days."

Broken Wing had been filled with pleasure at the few words of praise from her. *Storm was right*, she thought, *the Indians* are *warm, sensitive people.*

Next, Storm led her to the bunkhouse, where she was led on a complete tour.

The sleeping quarters appeared tidy and immaculate. Lazy Dog stood leaning against a broom handle, smiling proudly as Sarah commented on the room's cleanliness.

Next they moved to the large kitchen behind the bunkhouse. Manny, Emily, and Snakebite chopped vegetables for stew, while a large black caldron steamed over the fire.

Sarah commented on their efficiency, noting to herself how

perfectly Aunt Emily fit in, spending more time here with Manny than at the ranch house.

Next Storm showed her the large garden behind the bunkhouse. Eagle Eyes, Leo, Little Hawk, Bent Arrow, and Red Moon waved from various positions of planting, hoeing, weeding, and watering the spacious, neatly rowed garden.

"This is where all our vegetables and herbs come from," Storm explained.

Sarah knew the gardeners waited expectantly for her comment.

"I can't believe it!" Sarah proclaimed, shaking her head. "The rows are so neat and straight! I can't see even one weed! It's the most wonderful garden I've ever seen!"

Trying to act nonchalant over her praise, the men shifted their feet nervously, eyes downcast. Sarah caught some wide smiles before heads turned bashfully.

Sarah felt tears sting her eyes. Making them happy had been easy. As proud people the recognition and praise made them feel appreciated and important.

Glancing quickly at Storm, Sarah caught his look of pride, but not for the men, for her. "Thank you, Sarah. That meant a great deal to them," he said sincerely.

"I only say what I mean. You should know that by now."

He smiled broadly, "Yes, but I haven't decided yet whether it's an asset or liability!"

Waving to the men, they rode on toward the cattle grazing lands. They rode in silence until it dawned on Sarah that someone had been missing.

"Where's Black Feather?"

"Gone."

"What happened?"

"I had to let him go because of what happened with your saddle that day."

"You're sure then that he cut the strap?"

"He practically admitted it. Not at first, but after I persisted with the questioning he lost his temper and gave me what I needed, a motive. After that I had to fire him—you wouldn't have been safe here."

"What did he say? I have a right to know!" she demanded, seeing the closed look on his face.

"He feels you're a threat to Little Bird's happiness."

She spoke in a small, almost inaudible voice. "Oh, dear!"

"I *had* to fire him."

"Where did he go?" she asked.

"Back to the reservation, just over the river into Oklahoma."

"Are there many of your people there?"

"All that aren't here."

"What's the reservation like?" she asked as they approached an open area where hundreds of scattered cattle grazed leisurely.

"It's getting better. It was terrible at first. The government promised much but delivered little. They didn't know enough about Indians to help them. For instance, they insisted the Indians quit their teepees and live in huts and shacks. The Indians had to obey to get the much-needed food and supplies."

They stopped and Storm continued, leaning casually on his saddle horn. "Then, the Indians began falling sick, dropping like flies. Tuberculosis. We complained, until finally they came up with a solution. The government ordered them to move back into their teepees, realizing they needed the fresh air. So now they're back to the teepees.

"Next, they insisted Indians learn farming, but the Indians rebelled, especially the fierce warriors. You see, gardening had always been the Indian women's work. The men felt degraded. Our Indian agent, Tatum, a good Christian man, helped them get over that. Some he gave jobs raising cattle, like our crew here. Some more restless warriors were given jobs riding guard over the government supply wagons. It all worked out, but it took time."

"Can we do anything to help?" she asked.

"Sarah, I'm glad you asked that!" he exclaimed with a twinkle in his silvery eyes.

~~ 7 ~~

"Now that you're the owner," he gave her a sideways glance, "at least for now, I hope you'll continue with what your grandfather and I have done.

"We not only hire as many Indians from the reservation as we can, but give them cattle when we slaughter. We refuse them vegetables from our garden, though, because then they wouldn't work at their own. It's important that they try to be self-sufficient, but beef is difficult for them to acquire. The government allots some, but it never lasts the whole winter. Sometimes the shipments are up to six months late, and they practically starve. That's why we started helping them."

"My grandfather must have been a generous man."

"Yes, but he had other motives as well. During the first few years after the Indians were forced onto the reservation, every time the government went back on a promise or communications became mixed between here and Washington, the Indians would get angry and attack neighboring ranches. By befriending and hiring them, our ranch became a kind of sanctuary or neutral ground. They seldom bothered us, except to steal an occasional head of cattle or a few horses. Nothing like what was done to our neighbors!

"Things improved when the government sent us Lawrie Tatum. He came to Fort Sill in sixty-nine as agent for the Kiowa and Comanche tribes. He not only worked hard at pacifying and getting to know the Indians, he brought them the Word of God. A good man, Tatum brought them what they needed most, God. I'd ride over once a month and help with Bible lessons and Sunday school. Some mighty fine Indians turned out after Tatum gave them the Gospel. But it took him years to disband the Quahadas."

"Quahadas?" she asked.

"A small band of Comanches who refused to live on the reservation. They killed, pillaged, and kidnapped in this area for many years. Even we feared them. Fierce and ruthless, they wouldn't have hesitated attacking Arrow C; they were angry with the Indians who made peace with white men, as well as the white men."

"Are they still around?" she asked uncomfortably.

"Most have either died or moved to the reservation, but what they did to this community will never be forgotten, and every Indian is paying the penalty for it."

It rained the next morning. Sarah lazed around her room after breakfasting with a pouting Little Bird and a lovely but doting Dawn.

Pacing the floor nervously, she began straightening the dresser tops, for lack of something better to do, and found the book she'd brought down from the attic. *This is as good a time as any to read,* she thought, settling herself comfortably in one of the armchairs.

She opened the book to find not a printed novel, but a handwritten log of some sort. The name on the inside cover read *Elizabeth Epsom Greenly Clarke.* The first three names were written in faded ink, the last dark ink, as if added later.

She read the first page. Why, this was Elizabeth's diary! She looked at the dates. This Elizabeth was her grandmother! Interest renewed, she delved into the handwritten accounts of Elizabeth's journey from Louisiana to Texas, led by Stephen Austin. They left New Orleans by way of the Natchitochees in 1824, according to Elizabeth.

The travelers, all traders, had banded together for the mutual protection of their $35,000 worth of hardware, cutlery, hats, shirting, linen, hosiery, and other dry goods. There were eighty of them, Sarah read: two wagons, two carts, and twenty dearborns. Sarah wondered what a dearborn was, but on the next page Elizabeth described it as a light, four-wheeled covered wagon. This is what Elizabeth traveled in, with someone named Henry. Her brother perhaps?

Sarah reluctantly put the book down when Aunt Emily came bouncing in.

"Hello, my dear." She looked cheerful, with cheeks rosy and eyes bright.

"Don't you look chipper on such a dreary day!" Sarah greeted.

Emily sat daintily in the other chair, folded hands in her lap. "I've got news, and I figure you should be the first I tell, although Manny has already told Storm."

"I think I know." Sarah tried to suppress her delight.

"How could you?"

"How could I not? You and Manny have been together since the day we left Dodge City."

"It was that obvious?" she asked.

"It was. Shall I have Storm demand that Manny state his intentions?"

"That won't be necessary. Manny proposed last night, and I said yes."

"Aunt Emily! How wonderful! Wait until Mother hears!

She'll think us mad; you marrying a Mexican who was raised
Comanche, and me in love with a half-breed!"

"Don't forget to add, Sarah, dear—an uncle to boot."

Sarah frowned. "Hogwash. We're all related somewhere,
aren't we?"

"They say your children could be deformed or worse,"
Emily warned.

"Well, then we won't have any," she pouted. "It doesn't
appear we'll ever have to worry about that. He's still determined to marry Little Bird."

"Perhaps it's better in the long run, Sarah."

"How can you say that? I love him!"

"Well, we'll continue to pray for you both," Emily soothed.
"And we want you and Storm at our wedding. In fact, Storm
will perform the ceremony. We want no fuss, but Rosa will
probably make a feast out of it."

"I'm so happy for you." Sarah embraced her aunt. "Will
you live here with us?"

"No. Storm offered us the use of the hunting lodge in the
woods, about a mile away. We walked over there this
morning, in the rain; we were that excited! It's rustic, but I'm
sure I can make a wonderful home for Manny there."

Sarah embraced her aunt again. "It was kind of Storm to let
you *use* the lodge, but since this is *my* ranch, I veto the offer."
When Emily cocked her head curiously, Sarah continued,
"The lodge is my wedding gift to you and Manny."

Later, alone in the study, browsing through the bookkeeping records, Sarah felt close to Storm. His presence filled the
room. His coat hung on the doorknob, his watch lay propped
on the desk so he could see the time as he worked. She
recalled Dawn's words, that first day, when she'd asked
where Storm slept: "Storm sleeps in the bunkhouse usually,
although sometimes I find him on the couch in the study
after a long night working on the books."

Poor Storm! How hard he worked making the ranch run smoothly. Shouldn't she be doing something, contributing to the ranch in some way?

Suddenly an idea took root in Sarah's mind. If she could learn to keep the books, she would not only be helping the ranch, but Storm, who worked too hard already.

She picked up Storm's watch and rubbed it against her cheek, smiling.

Dawn entered with a tray. "I brought tea. May I join you?"

"Of course. Had any luck searching for the will?"

"No. Have you?" asked Dawn.

"An old book and plenty of old clothes were all I found."

Dawn took a seat on a nearby chair, frowned, and jumped up. Grabbing a paper from the desk, she hastily folded it to place under the chair leg.

"Dawn, that paper was the receipt from the cattle purchase in Dodge City; Storm will need it!"

"Oh," Dawn straightened it somewhat and handed it back. "Sorry. It's a terrible habit, grabbing paper without thinking. Storm gets so angry with me."

"Here, take this." Sarah offered her scrap paper.

"Thank you. I have an aversion to wobbly furniture."

They laughed over the incident and excitedly made plans for the upcoming wedding, like two young schoolgirls.

Afterwards, Sarah returned to her room to dress for dinner but found herself absorbed in the diary instead.

Elizabeth wrote about the people with whom she traveled. Confusingly, she named Wilson Clarke as a fellow trader traveling with a load of hardware, while she and Henry had linens.

But that didn't make sense! *Unless*, Sarah mused, *they were both single*. She concluded they probably met on this journey. How romantic! Realizing she would soon be late for dinner, she finally put the book down to dress, thinking the whole time of the romantic way her grandparents had met.

*   *   *

That night at supper, Dawn noticed the table was shaky and reached for a scrap of paper. This time she grabbed Storm's notes lying near his plate and prepared to place them under the table leg.

"Hey!" Storm yelled. "I need those! They're lists of cattle to be branded!"

"Oh. Sorry," she said simply, returning the paper.

"We must teach her to read," growled Storm. "Mother, you must have moved the table while you were cleaning," he said, pushing the table a few inches. "See, now it doesn't wobble."

Early the next morning Sarah helped Dawn prepare the living room for the wedding. They were placing large vases of fragrant flowers, which Joseph and Rosa had picked, in strategic places.

"How's this, Dawn?" Sarah asked, setting down a large pot of dew-tipped red roses near the stairway. "Oh, the vase wobbles here. The floor is uneven."

"They look perfect there. Let me fix them." She grabbed the nearest paper, which happened to be Manny and Emily's wedding-party menu, left on the fireplace mantel for Sarah to approve.

"No! Dawn!" Sarah screamed, running to rescue the paper. "This is important," she said softly, seeing the hurt in Dawn's large brown eyes.

An idea that had been growing in Sarah's mind finally matured. Excitedly, she grabbed Dawn's arm. "Dawn, did you fix any furniture in the study or my bedroom since Wilson took sick or died?"

"Probably, I do it all the time. The floors in this house are uneven, and it drives me crazy when the furniture rocks."

"Let's go into the study; show me everything you fixed like that." Sarah led her by the hand.

"I fixed the cabinet, there." She pointed.

Sarah rushed to the cabinet, pulling out the wad of paper. "Dawn, there are *three* papers here!" she exclaimed in disbelief.

"Well," she said, "it was a big wobble."

After checking the papers, Sarah replaced them. "Where else?"

"The desk, both left legs," she admitted.

Sarah pulled the papers from both legs. One was a newspaper page, the other some sort of legal document. "The will!" she shouted, suddenly recognizing it.

"Sh-h-h," Dawn quieted her. "Little Bird mustn't hear."

Sarah hugged Dawn, "We found the will! And it's all due to you!"

"But it was my foolishness that lost it to begin with," Dawn lamented.

"Yes, but had it not been lost, I wouldn't be here, and Storm would be confined to a loveless marriage."

"Then I did good." She smiled.

"You did good," agreed Sarah, hugging her. She scanned the paper, noting that not only did Storm indeed own the ranch, but the will *had* been drawn up by Samuel Lewis!

"What should we do with the will now?" Dawn asked.

"Why don't we put it back under the desk leg? I can't think of a better hiding place, but from now on I'll give you scrap paper to put under furniture, understood?" Sarah asked, grinning.

There was no music, yet in Sarah's eyes the wedding couldn't have been more beautiful. Manny stood before the fireplace, looking up, as Emily came down the stairs wearing a bright-blue ruffled dress. Sarah had arranged her aunt's white hair with daisies to form a crown. Emily Ruggles appeared regal, marching proudly and staring lovingly into her future husband's eyes. Sarah, dressed in a pink bustled dress from her Chicago wardrobe, followed, holding the train of her aunt's dress.

Storm stood beside Manny, holding his Book. Sarah and Storm's eyes locked as she walked behind her aunt. Sarah knew their thoughts were in accord: This could be their wedding and her walking down the stairs to meet him, instead of Emily to meet Manny. If only it could be!

Emily and Manny stood solemnly before Storm as he read from the Bible. He then recited the traditional wedding vows before pronouncing them man and wife. Manny was now her great-uncle!

As expected Rosa had a feast ready, and tables were set up outside. The whole crew came, with best manners and Sunday clothes. Everyone felt merry, and the yard echoed with laughter and gaiety.

Little Bird claimed Storm for the day, clutching his arm possessively, leaving Sarah with Hunter and Dawn. Storm's body may have been piloted around by Little Bird, but his eyes remained on Sarah, saving her good spirit. Sarah knew Storm had to do what he was doing. Storm was a man of principles, a man of his word. Weren't those the very qualities she had fallen in love with in the first place?

Sarah's burden had also been lightened by her daily talks to God. How wonderful she felt afterwards! She trusted what she read in the Bible Storm had given her, and she wrote a verse on paper and tucked it under her pillow: "The Lord is nigh unto all them that call upon him . . ." (Psalms 145:18).

Sarah's Bible readings also managed to tickle her conscience, making her feel guilty about deceiving Storm. What would God want her to do? Be honest, even if it wrecked Storm's life? What about Little Bird? Didn't she have a right to happiness? And what about the ranch? According to the new will, she wasn't the owner. By keeping silent and hiding it, she was committing fraud, stealing from the man she loved. She vowed to spend more time in prayer, for she needed answers that only God could provide.

After her usual morning ride, Sarah bathed and donned one of her comfortable homespun dresses, a buttercup yellow that perfectly matched her hair.

Taking her Bible, she sat down for her morning devotions, a habit she had gotten into since the day Storm had showed her how to commit her life to God. She cherished the Bible he'd given her, since it had been his very own. He had marked certain verses, written explanations to some passages in his own hand. These were helpful to Sarah, a beginner.

She spent considerable time in prayer that morning, asking God to help her do the right thing.

As usual, after talking with God, she felt confident, exhilarated, and full of love for everyone. She knew what had to be done today and went in search of Little Bird.

Sarah knocked on the Indian girl's bedroom door. It opened slowly; Little Bird's black eyes peeked out then widened and froze at the sight of Sarah.

"Hello, Little Bird," Sarah said, trying to act casual. "Could I come in? I'd like to talk to you, if I may?"

After a pause—which seemed to Sarah like an hour, but was actually only a few moments—Little Bird reluctantly opened the door wider and stepped back, allowing her to enter.

Closing the door carefully behind her, Sarah sighed. "I thought it time we became better acquainted."

Little Bird said nothing but remained stiff, standing by the door as if ready to take flight.

Thinking the girl might be frightened of her, Sarah said gently, "Come, Little Bird, sit with me." She pointed to a pair of wooden chairs.

Little Bird shook her head and snapped, "You want talk? Talk. I stay here."

"Very well. Do you mind if I sit?" Sarah lowered herself

into one of the chairs. "It feels friendlier to chat sitting. Sure you won't join me?"

The Indian girl shook her head.

"Little Bird," Sarah hesitated, folding and unfolding her hands on her lap. "I'd like to be your friend."

Little Bird seemed to relax a bit but remained stationed at the door.

"With the baby coming, I'm sure you could use a friend. I could help prepare for it. Would you like that?"

Little Bird's hand went automatically to her enlarged midriff.

Sarah, confident that Little Bird was softening, continued. "I love babies. I wonder if it's a boy or a girl?"

Little Bird smiled coldly, "Baby is boy, like father."

"But how do you know?" asked Sarah.

"Just know."

"I see," Sarah said thoughtfully. It wouldn't do to argue. "Do you have baby clothes? Have you made any plans for him?"

Little Bird shook her head. Did Sarah detect a touch of fear behind those beautiful, dark eyes? What was Little Bird afraid of?

"We could make some lovely things for him. I'm just fair with a needle and thread, but wait until Aunt Emily begins sewing for him!" Sarah glanced around the room. "Don't you have a cradle for him to sleep in either? When is the baby due?"

Again Sarah saw fear in Little Bird's eyes as she said, "Baby will come next moon."

"Next moon?" Sarah repeated. "But that's only a few weeks away! We had better get busy. I'll recruit Aunt Emily's help as soon as she and Manny are finished honeymooning."

"Honeymooning?" Little Bird looked puzzled.

"Yes," said Sarah. "That's what married couples do after the ceremony. They spend time alone—getting to know each other without being bothered. Some go away on a trip, others just stay locked away for a while. It's very romantic, don't you think?"

"I will tell Storm," pronounced Little Bird, with childlike eyes wide. "I want honeymooning, too."

Sarah forced a smile. "I'll see what I have in my trunk to begin your baby's layette. We'll see about getting you a cradle, too."

Sarah walked to the door where Little Bird stood. "If you need anything, Little Bird, come to me. I'll help you."

~ 8 ~

The blazing Texas sun bore down relentlessly, searing and withering everything within its fiery realm.

Sarah and Rosa sympathized with Storm and the crew, who worked in the suffocating heat, building a fence for the grazing cattle. Deciding cool lemonade would refresh them, the two women scoured a large pail and filled it with sweetened lemon juice and cool, pure spring water.

Sarah rejoiced that Rosa was strong enough to carry the pail to the buckboard with little effort and that Broken Wing had agreed to drive the buckboard to where the men worked. Sarah sat behind with the lemonade, making sure none spilled.

As they approached the workers, one looked up curiously. Recognizing Sarah, he nudged the next man, who in turn alerted another, until all were waving and smiling. Even Storm seemed pleased by her surprise visit.

Sitting on the wagon bed, Sarah scooped lemonade into tin cups and handed them to the sweating men.

A welcome treat, the men drank until the ladle resounded loudly against the empty bucket's bottom. Storm ordered a rest, and the laborers sprawled beneath the shade of a giant cottonwood tree while he joined Sarah upon the wagon.

"This is some treat. Was it your idea?" Storm asked, draining his cup.

"Rosa and I thought you men deserved some refreshment, working so hard in this unbearable heat."

"Very thoughtful—and greatly appreciated."

Sarah smiled. "I had a talk with Little Bird this morning."

"And?" he raised his eyebrows inquisitively.

"And I tried to make friends."

"Did you succeed?" he asked, wiping his perspiring face with a handkerchief.

"I don't know. I offered to help her prepare for the baby. This seemed to please her, yet she didn't exactly bubble with enthusiasm. I'll keep trying."

"Why?" He stared at her intently.

"Because you and God taught me to love my enemies."

He smiled and winked his approval.

"But why did you agree to marry Little Bird, knowing you didn't love her?" Sarah looked at him imploringly.

His smile faded. He shrugged. "I did what I thought right at the time. I still think it's the proper thing to do, but it seemed like a better idea then, before I met you." He looked away quickly and continued, "I was always fond of Little Bird. After my father died, she came to me in tears, admitting what had happened. Her family, except her brother, disowned her in shame. She had nowhere to go and no future for herself or the baby. Living here among Indians, I figured I'd probably end up marrying one anyway, so why not Little Bird? I then gave her my word that as soon as the ranch became legally mine, I'd marry her."

After silently considering his explanation a moment, Sarah blurted, "I have another—"

Storm cut off her words with laughter.

"What's so funny?" she asked, looking about for the object of his merriment.

"It's you," he groaned between snorts of glee. "The crew finally found an Indian name for you. I was suddenly reminded just how fitting it is!"

"My Indian name?" she asked anxiously. "What is it?"

"Curious Eyes," he chuckled.

"Curious Eyes! Me?"

"All you do is ask questions. The Indians say they can see the question before you ask, because your blue eyes grow wide and round. They're right," he exclaimed gleefully. "And I see another question coming now—but we've got to get back to work."

Sobering, he set down his empty tin cup and hopped off the wagon. "But Storm," she pouted, "I still have my question to ask."

"All right, ask, but hurry, we've got work to do."

"If the second will means so much to you, why aren't you searching for it?"

Storm picked up one of her hands, brought it to his lips, and kissed it. "That was a good question, Sarah. Now hurry back to the ranch, so I can work." He picked up his tools and walked toward the fence, gesturing the men back to work.

"But Storm," she called. "You didn't answer my question!"

"I said you could ask, not that I'd answer. Bye, Sarah!" He nodded to Broken Wing, who then turned the wagon around and headed back to the ranch, with a pouting Sarah sitting behind him.

Feet dangling, she sat on the back of the wagon bed, replaying her conversation with Storm in her mind. Would she ever understand him? Why didn't he continue searching for the will? Why did Storm always manage to evade her questions? She chuckled to herself as she recalled her new Indian name. Curious Eyes—she rather liked it!

She watched Storm and the crew disappear behind trees as the dirt trail curved away from them toward the woods, which separated the work crew from the ranch house.

The thick forest and wild brush lined the road on both

sides, and its cool shade felt glorious as she leaned back to let its full benefit embrace her body. A sudden movement on her left jerked her back to a sitting position, alarmed.

A figure darted from the thicket and crossed the road to a footpath that led to the house. Sarah quickly recognized Little Bird's swollen form, but before she could think what the Indian girl might be doing in the woods, another figure leaped out, grabbing Little Bird by the arm. A man appeared to be telling her about something he'd forgotten, because he then turned and ran back into the same brush he'd leaped from, and Little Bird continued walking sedately along the narrow footpath.

Sarah had recognized Black Feather instantly by his long hair. Hunter claimed Storm had warned Black Feather several times to cut his hair, but Black Feather had refused. Because he was Little Bird's brother, Storm had excused his disobedience—temporarily.

Sarah decided not to let it bother her that Black Feather sneaked to see his sister. Perhaps they were close, and what harm could it do?

But as the wagon bumped along the remainder of the way home, questions darted through Sarah's mind. Should she tell Storm about seeing Black Feather and Little Bird? Would Storm call out the men to search for his future brother-in-law? What purpose would be served by telling him? What harm would it do if she didn't?

After supper that night, Sarah detained Storm as he headed for the bunkhouse. "Storm, wait. I need a word with you."

"More questions, Curious Eyes?" he grinned.

Noticing Little Bird's eyes jealously flaming, Sarah suggested, with a nod, that they talk in the study.

Closing the door carefully, Sarah leaned against the oak portal and decided against telling him about seeing Black Feather. Instead she said, "Storm, I need something to do."

"Can't you just sit around and look pretty?" he asked, standing beside her.

"This is my ranch," she said, in a weaker voice than she would have before finding the second will, "and I'd like to help run it."

He studied her. "You're serious, aren't you?"

"Very."

"What do you want to do, work on the fence? Or help Broken Wing with the horses?" he asked calmly, with one raised eyebrow.

"Couldn't I take over the book work?" she asked apprehensively.

"Have you ever done bookkeeping before?"

"No. But I'm willing to learn." She waited eagerly for his reply.

Rolling his eyes, he sighed, then walked to the desk. "Come here then. I'll show you what to do." Sarah thought that beneath his show of impatience, he seemed relieved. Was he glad that the books were all she had asked to take over?

While she knew the ranch wasn't actually hers, it *had* belonged to her grandfather, which she felt entitled her to something. So after that evening, Sarah kept the books and did the monthly payroll, which kept her occupied and gave her an active hand in the ranch. It also warmed her to know that Storm would no longer have to toil over the books into the early morning hours.

When Sarah wasn't working on the books, she helped Dawn run the house, which was no small task. She also sewed for Little Bird's baby or visited Aunt Emily. Her grandmother's diary was forgotten, until one night when the suffocating heat kept her awake.

After much restless tossing, Sarah remembered the diary. With a sigh, she parted the mosquito netting and tiptoed to her bureau for the worn book. Returning to bed, she carefully lit the lamp, propped up the pillows, and found the marked place in the diary.

After reading two pages, Sarah gasped. She had discovered Henry was not Elizabeth's brother, but her husband! If that wasn't shocking enough, Elizabeth spoke of her concern for their unborn child. What did this mean? Sarah read on, turning the leaves impatiently while Elizabeth wrote pages and pages on nothing significant.

Then frantic penmanship told of Henry's accident during a river crossing. Her young husband, guiding the team and wagon through swift-moving water, lost his footing and drowned. Elizabeth poured her grief into the next several pages.

Elizabeth not only mourned her husband but feared her helplessness in continuing without him. She couldn't do the jobs required of each wagon owner, especially in her condition. Yet she couldn't turn back. Elizabeth desperately demanded of her diary, "Where shall I go? What shall become of me and my baby?"

Then Elizabeth wrote of the kindnesses of Wilson Clarke, a bachelor, traveling in the wagon behind hers. "Were it not for Mr. Clarke," she wrote, "I would never have survived those first few weeks without Henry."

The next entry thoroughly shocked Sarah. "Wilson and I married today. We aren't in love, but it's the practical thing to do."

Sarah gasped.

If Elizabeth's baby turned out to be a boy named Thomas, then she was not Wilson Clarke's granddaughter!

Sarah flipped the pages, scanning each anxiously, searching for the page announcing the baby's birth. She had to discover if her father was that baby—Henry's baby!

There it was, toward the end of the book:

June 5, 1824. Somewhere near Jacinto, Texas. Today I did not grieve, but felt joy. I held my newborn son for the first time. He was born yesterday, but I felt too ill and tired to hold or enjoy him. Mrs. Warren, the midwife, said I'd given them quite a scare. Now I feel weak but happy, holding Thomas Henry. I'd planned to name him Henry Thomas, but Wilson explained it would be better for our new life in Texas if no one knew Thomas was not his. I agreed. From now on, there will be no looking back.

Sarah threw the book down and blew out her lamp.

There it was! She had no right here and had no claim on the ranch—with or without the second will. What should she do now? Continue to cheat Storm out of his inheritance? Tell him the truth and let him marry Little Bird?

Sarah prayed, there in the dark, until she finally fell asleep. But upon awakening in the morning, the memory of her discovery spurred her into action. She hastily dressed for riding and left the house.

Bypassing her quiet place by the brook, Sarah rode straight to Emily and Manny's cottage.

Pounding on the heavy wooden cottage door, Sarah hoped Manny wasn't home. He might not appreciate her visit at this hour of the morning.

The door was opened, finally, by a sleepy-eyed Aunt Emily. Still in her nightgown, she peeked around the half-open door.

"Oh, Sarah, it's you! Come in!"

"Sorry to bother you so early—but this is an emergency."

"You're welcome anytime. Hurry in, dear," she invited, opening the door wide. "Sit here," she pointed to the rustic wooden table with four hand-carved chairs neatly arranged around it. "I'll make us some tea. You just missed Manny. He left ten minutes ago."

When comfortably sipping tea at the cozy kitchen table, Sarah confided her discovery, then asked bluntly if Emily had known about her father's parentage the whole time.

"Absolutely not! I wonder if your father even knew!" Emily exclaimed. "And if your mother knew, she never confided in me."

"Do you think father knew and that's why he hardly spoke of my gran—I mean Wilson Clarke?" asked Sarah.

"Could be. No way of knowing. Does this mean you must give up the ranch?" Emily asked, setting her shaking teacup back into its saucer.

"I don't know what to do," Sarah cried, wringing her napkin tightly as she spoke. "If you promise not to tell anyone, even Manny, I'll tell you another secret." When her aunt nodded, she continued. "Dawn and I found the second will. It does exist. Wilson Clarke did leave the ranch to his son, his only son, Storm."

"Oh, dear!" exclaimed Emily, hands flying to her face.

"But," Sarah said quietly, "Dawn made me promise not to tell Storm that we found it. She doesn't want Storm to marry Little Bird either."

Sarah sighed. "Now I don't know what to do! Should I keep the ranch and Storm? Or let them both go? I can't do one without the other."

"Well," said Emily knowingly, "it not being your secret alone, you had better talk it over with Dawn as soon as possible. 'Never put off till tomorrow what can be done today,' " she quoted, making Sarah smile despite her woes.

"There is, however, a good side to this, my dear," her aunt clucked. "It means Storm is not a blood relative of yours. Your children won't be—"

"Aunt Emily! I hadn't even thought about that! Though it does me no good, for Storm still believes I am, and if I tell him otherwise, I not only lose the ranch, but most important, him. I lose to a loveless marriage," she said, pounding her fist upon the table in desperation.

Then Sarah grabbed her aunt's hand. "Promise me you won't tell Manny. Not yet, please?"

*　　*　　*

Sarah had noticed a change in Little Bird lately. She seemed warmer to Sarah and sought her out often. Sarah didn't know what had brought on this sudden friendliness, but as Aunt Emily had told her when they'd discussed it, "Never look a gift horse in the mouth."

Sarah thought that Little Bird's turnabout might be due to their interest in her baby. She and Aunt Emily had made a full basket of clothing, and Little Bird cooed over each tiny garment.

Because of Little Bird's now being under foot constantly, Sarah hadn't yet spoken to Dawn about her discovery from the diary. She had to be sure of Little Bird's whereabouts before discussing anything so crucial.

Sarah also had few personal confrontations with Storm. Even when he helped with the books, he stuck to business. It seemed to Sarah that whenever his eyes grew soft and she thought their romantic relationship would reopen, he would excuse himself quickly on some pretense of an errand.

Storm and the crew continued their hard work on the fence that they boasted would be two miles long when completed. Storm explained it as the newest method for ranchers to keep their herds together for easy roundup and to keep them safe from rustlers.

Sarah and Emily finally sat and carefully worded a letter to Sarah's mother. If Agnes Clarke stopped home after her European trip, instead of going directly to the Centennial Exposition in Philadelphia, which she had planned to visit, she would receive the letter in a few weeks. Of course they hadn't mentioned Wilson Clarke's secret or Storm. But Emily's marriage story had to be told. They wondered how Agnes would respond to that!

Surprisingly, writing to Agnes Clarke and thinking of home hadn't given Sarah or Emily an ounce of homesickness. Firmly rooted in Texas were Emily's life and Sarah's heart.

*   *   *

Sunday soon became Sarah's favorite day at the ranch. She enjoyed the services and later the fellowship of the others, who could enjoy light socializing, unhurried by their usual duties.

As Storm had promised, no one at Arrow C worked on Sunday. Even Rosa, who prepared Sunday's simple meals on Saturday, relaxed in a rocking chair on the front porch each Sunday.

Yet Sarah grew restless. The more she read her Bible, went to church services, and sang praises to God, the more her conscience nagged her.

She knew she was doing wrong, yet because of her love, couldn't do otherwise. She also knew if this strain continued, she'd soon buckle and give up everything. But how fond she'd grown not only of Storm but of the ranch, Dawn, Rosa, and the whole crew. How could she leave all this?

Fortunately, keeping busy helped Sarah keep her mind from her dilemma. She and Aunt Emily continued making baby clothes, and Red Moon made a wooden cradle. Little Bird often sat for hours, smoothing the wood and rocking it gently. She would fondle each nightgown and sweater made for her baby. Sarah often caught Little Bird gazing at her strangely, as if puzzled by Sarah's benevolence, yet other times Little Bird's looks toward her revealed barefaced contempt.

One evening Little Bird's biting sarcasm and poison-arrow glares became too much for Sarah, so she decided to retire early. She climbed the stairs, feeling the stabbing pain in her back from Little Bird's sharp, hateful black eyes. A quick glance behind her, when she reached the landing, confirmed the sensation. She couldn't get to her room fast enough, it seemed. Finally, she slipped soundlessly between her door and frame, resting her head back against the closed wooden portal.

Eyes closed, she sighed. A sound caused her blue eyes to

fly open and anxiously scan the room by the orange light of the fast-fading evening sunset. A stooped figure at the foot of her bed straightened slowly and turned toward her in embarrassment.

"Storm!" she gasped. "Whatever are you doing here?" Noting that the quilt's corner had been lifted, the bureau drawers left partially opened, and that the closet door stood ajar, she came to her own conclusions.

Sarah tapped her foot impatiently. "So you're finally hunting for the will. I can assure you, I've searched this room completely. Is Little Bird becoming impatient for her husband?"

"I wasn't looking for the will," he stated firmly.

"What then?" she demanded, foot still tapping, arms akimbo.

He approached her, placing his hands on her shoulders. "I was making sure your room was—ah—safe."

"Safe? Oh, come, Storm. You can do better than that." Probably because of her own guilty conscience, she blurted an accusation at him. "You think I found the will and have it hidden here!"

Moving his hands from her shoulders to his pockets, he said softly, "No. I know you'd never do anything like that."

Sarah gulped and prepared to confess everything. He trusted her! How could she do this to him? On the verge of confessing the truth, her mind suddenly fled from her guilt and focused on his explanation.

"I guess, having been caught in the act, I owe you an honest answer." He shuffled his feet uncomfortably. "Several of the crew have spotted Black Feather on the property, and that worries us. They say he likes revenge. He's one Indian I've not been able to get through to at all."

"You were looking for Black Feather here? In my room?" she asked, disbelief apparent in her impatient tone.

"No, silly." He cuffed her chin lightly. "I thought he might put something harmful in here. Something deadly, like a snake or spider. The crew hinted at some of his methods."

Sarah gasped fearfully. "You think he might? Did you look all over?"

"The room is safe. But if you don't mind, I'd like to sleep in the next room for a few nights. Mother can sleep in the room Emily left." He walked to the door. "If you need me, just holler."

"Storm. . . ," she faltered contritely, "I'm—"

"No apologies—I would have thought the same in your place. Good night." He winked and was gone before Sarah could thank him.

✎ 9 ✎

*D*ressed in the borrowed pants and a soft, Victorian-collared white blouse, Sarah mounted Red early the next morning and headed for her favorite spot. Breathing in the fresh, crisp morning air, she sighed—she would miss this place!

Loping toward the stream, a sudden noise stunned her into halting Red. Something had whizzed by her head. She heard the sound again and swung her head around. Flame-tipped pain seared through her forehead. Her hand shot to her temple. It felt wet—blood! Dazed, Sarah fell from her horse into soft, cushioning bushes.

The sound of hoofbeats approaching caused her to freeze in her awkward position. Was her attacker coming to finish the job?

As the rider came into better view, Sarah sighed with relief and threw her head back on the flowering mattress that had caught her. Storm!

Bounding off his horse, he ran to her. "Are you all right? What happened?"

"It's just a scratch. I was hit with something, by someone."

Touching her bloodied temple lightly, her face twitched in pain.

"Sure you're all right?" Storm asked, his worried gray eyes inspecting her anxiously.

She nodded.

He remounted. "Stay right there. Don't move!" He rode off in the direction she'd been traveling.

Being immobile and having little choice in the matter, Sarah obeyed. Her middle had sunk so low into the bush she couldn't get enough leverage to hoist herself out of her haven anyway.

Soon Storm returned, frowning. "Your attacker left no trail. Definitely an Indian! Probably Black Feather. I knew he was up to something. That's why I followed you." He sighed. "This is all my fault."

"If you'll just help me out of this shrubbery, I'll forgive you," Sarah quipped impatiently.

Strong hands gripped her trim waist, lifted her effortlessly, and set her down upon her feet. She swayed slightly. His hands tightened, steadying her. Whenever they were this close, she felt drawn to him as the livestock were drawn to the Cimarron River after four days without water.

She searched his eyes. Yes, he felt it, too. Would the power of their magnetism overcome them yet again? But no, he donned his disciplined look. Holding her at arm's length, he asked brusquely, "Will you be all right, or are you going to faint on me?"

"You can let go of me," she snapped. "I won't faint. I know my nearness repulses you, which is probably why you've been avoiding me. Go ahead, let go!" She shrugged his hands from her shoulders.

"You know that's not true, Sarah. Quite the contrary. But one of us has to be strong."

"Why? Why, Storm? Why can't you let things fall into place? Can't you simply tell Little Bird—"

"Sarah, we've been over this. Now let's get you to the house. That cut needs attention. Looks like you were clipped by a small rock."

She planted her feet firmly, crossing her arms across her chest. "I refuse to go with you. I can be stubborn, too!"

With an amusing look Storm said, "And you think I can't move you?" Stepping toward her, he swept her up and placed her on his horse. Climbing up behind her, he said, "Now, let's find Red."

She leaned back, snuggling playfully against his broad chest.

"This is much better than walking!"

"Sarah! What am I to do with you?" he sighed, gently pushing her forward. "My mother is sure God sent you to me, but I'm thinking it's Satan's doing, the way you act! The Bible warns: 'For the lips of a strange woman drop as an honeycomb, and her mouth is smoother than oil: But her end is bitter as wormwood, sharp as a twoedged sword.' "

"You think that about me? I belong to God, Storm! Does Little Bird share your God? Perhaps she's the strange woman with honey dropping from her lips! Stop this horse," she fumed. "I prefer to walk!"

Sliding off the nearly halted horse, she stomped off on foot, without a backward glance.

"Sarah," he called, riding after her. "I'm sorry."

She forgave him instantly but was reluctant to let him out of his noose so quickly. She kept walking.

When she heard his horse running behind her, she wondered what he intended but refused to turn and look.

Suddenly, with one strong arm, he scooped her off the ground and placed her in front of him on the saddle. "I want you here," he whispered, nuzzling her ear, "where you belong."

"Then, why. . . ," she asked. Tears stung her eyes.

He stopped the horse. "I want to be fair with you." He

tenderly wiped a tear from her cheek with his index finger and spoke in a gentle, low voice that instantly soothed her. "Come, let's sit down somewhere and talk."

Helping her off the horse, he asked attentively, "Are you sure your head is all right?"

She nodded. "I'd forgotten all about it."

"Come then." He led her by the hand to a large shade tree.

While she made herself comfortable beneath the large, leafed branches, Storm wet his handkerchief from a canteen hanging from his saddle.

"Here." He held the cloth to her head gently. "This may help."

"You said you'd be fair. That will help more," she replied.

He dotted her wound with the fabric, making her wince. "What I'm doing is good for this wound, yet it hurts, doesn't it?" His voice was low and gentle but insistent. "It's the same with what I have to tell you. It'll be best in the long run, but it's going to hurt now. Do you understand, Sarah?"

She nodded, mesmerized by his soothing tone and sincere eyes.

Like a velvet murmur, his voice continued. "I don't find putting my arms around you repulsive. Just the opposite. Whenever I'm near you all I think of is holding you, kissing you, and making you mine. I think of the sweetness we've shared and the honest expression of your heart. How easy it would be to give in to my desires, but that wouldn't be fair. I have nothing to offer. I'm bound by a promise I must keep.

"You're a beautiful, vibrant young woman, and if things were different. . . . But they aren't. Stolen kisses here and there aren't fair to you, me, or Little Bird. I'm pledged to her and have no right romancing you or any other woman. You see, it's a dead end for us, Sarah. Please, help me keep my word and my honor."

"Giving me up isn't so difficult for you, is it, Storm?"

"Sarah," he whispered gruffly, tilting up her chin, his eyes piercing hers, "it's the hardest thing I've ever had to do."

The love in his eyes made her heart glow with warmth.

"Why does that make me feel better? It shouldn't. I want you happy." Sarah sighed and searched Storm's eyes. "I love you, Storm." Tears choked her voice. "I'll never love anyone the way I love you."

"Sarah, I want to speak words of love, too, but that would only make things harder." He held her face between his hands. "But I will tell you this much. Since returning from Dodge, I haven't been searching for the will, though I know it's in that house somewhere. Do you know why?"

She shook her head.

"Because, now I'm afraid I'll find it."

"Storm!" Her tear-laden eyelashes flew up.

"Stalling, giving God more time is all." He spoke in a matter-of-fact but gentle tone. "And you said something in anger a moment ago that may be the key I'm looking for in knowing for sure what God wants for me. *I don't know if Little Bird belongs to God.* God wouldn't want me to marry an unbeliever. Little Bird goes through all the motions, yet . . . I don't know. The baby's due anytime. I can't wait much longer. But remember, God will always come first in my life. If only I knew for sure what He wants me to do. I thought I knew before, but now. . . ." He shook his head in helpless confusion.

"I think I understand," she whispered compassionately.

Storm patted her hand, and his face softened with concern.

"Will you go back to the house with me now and have that cut fixed?" he asked, stroking her hair lightly.

"Storm. . . ," she faltered, gazing up into his warm, gray eyes. "I understand . . . now. I promise not to tease, but could we have one more intimate moment to remember for all time?"

Storm's answer was immediate. His lips descended on hers gently. Though the kiss was urgent and desperate, being their last, it remained untainted by any emotion or motivations other than pure, unadulterated love.

They returned to the house with an unspoken agreement, one that had been sealed with a kiss to remember forever.

Thanks to Storm, Sarah now had a bodyguard. Her faithful servant—and proud of the honor—Snakebite, now followed her wherever she went.

Entering the sun-filled dining room that first morning with her bodyguard, she found Dawn alone and greeted her.

"I heard about your companion." Dawn smiled.

"I'm flattered by Storm's concern." Sarah helped herself to coffee and toast from the sideboard.

Dawn stared thoughtfully at Sarah. "It pleases me, too, but. . . ," her eyes darted furtively about the room for unwelcome ears. "We must do something about Little Bird! Her time draws closer. Storm is determined to. . . ."

"Wait!" Sarah cautioned. "Let's take a walk in the meadow. I, also, have something to discuss that mustn't be overheard."

Dawn nodded. Sarah finished her coffee, rose from the table, and lead the way, with Storm's mother following and Snakebite hurrying to keep up.

Strolling casually across the field of gently waving wild growth, Sarah stopped and looked about. She was glad Snakebite lingered behind them. Now she could talk to Dawn.

Standing in the middle of the field, Sarah felt like a ship at sea, surrounded by an ocean of flowing weeds and wildflowers. "So what's your news?" Dawn prompted, hands on hips.

"I read my grandmother's diary; I found her secret," she admitted, the breeze gently blowing loose tendrils of her fair hair.

"Oh, that!" Dawn disregarded her confession with a wave of her hand.

"You knew that I wasn't Wilson's granddaughter?"

116

"Of course. Wilson and I kept no secrets. He asked me not to mention it; I didn't."

"Not even to save the ranch for your son?"

"Storm forbade me to say anything!"

"*Storm knows, too?*"

"*I* didn't tell him," Dawn assured her. "Wilson did. They were close, and he wanted Storm to know he was his only true offspring."

"But Storm could have used that against me!"

"Storm said the Lord would take care of it and that it would not be right to use such a personal matter for material gain."

Sarah's heart swelled with love for Storm. "You both knew I wasn't Wilson's granddaughter?" Sarah asked in astonishment. "But you realize I can't keep quiet about the will we found any longer. Dawn, Storm trusts me! He's so good. I can't deceive him! I love him. . . . What am I to do?"

Dawn remained adamant. "If you love him, keep the secret. Why chase him into Little Bird's clutches? Besides, I may have something to help win our case."

As Sarah's face brightened Dawn continued, "Don't get excited. It may be nothing. It's just a hunch, and I can't say until I know more. I need time."

Sarah's spirit sank. "Something we have little of, by the looks of Little Bird."

As they strolled back toward the house Sarah touched Dawn's arm lightly. "Dawn, may I ask you a personal question?"

The Indian woman nodded with a gentle, motherly smile.

"Doesn't it upset you that your husband got . . . did . . . I mean. . . ." Sarah faltered.

"Fathered Little Bird's child? No. Because I insisted. It's all my fault," Dawn admitted sadly.

"You? But why?"

"This may be hard for you to understand, but growing up as a Comanche, my father had three wives, yet we had a

117

good family life. My mother lived with the other wives happily. They loved one another. Storm and his Bible say I'm wrong, and I have begun to see that is true. But then I felt it unnatural for Wilson to deprive me of the fellowship and help of other wives.

"Wilson felt as Storm does; we fought about this for years. Although our marriage was only recognized among the Indians, Wilson said we were married before the eyes of God, and that was good enough for him. He never took another wife, so I had no 'sisters' and no help with the chores. At that time we had only Rosa.

"So when Little Bird confessed that Wilson had fathered her child, I assumed he had finally been persuaded to take another wife. But I never thought he would skip the ceremony or not tell me about it. I guess he just didn't understand Indian customs."

Sarah shook her head. "But weren't you jealous? I couldn't stand the thought of Storm with another woman—that's why I must leave before the wedding."

"If you had lived with this custom, you wouldn't feel that way." Dawn turned around to look at Snakebite, who followed behind at a distance, rolling his eyes and sighing loudly. "We're walking too slowly for your chaperon; he's becoming impatient."

They both laughed at Snakebite's restlessness but increased their pace until they reached the house. Sarah asked, "Was Wilson as close to God as Storm is?"

"No, not as close as Storm. He often seemed interested and encouraged Storm but didn't get deeply involved with God until shortly before he died."

"And you? Have you God's Spirit within you?" Sarah asked hopefully.

Dawn's face glowed and her eyes glimmered. "Yes, Wilson, Storm, and I prayed together while he lay on his deathbed. He died happy, and while I miss him, I never grieve, because the Book assures me Wilson is with God."

She smiled, "I'm trying to learn everything about God and His Book, but it's hard for me because of my heritage. It's so very different."

"I'm learning the Bible, too. We can work on it together. Every day we'll read and study." Sarah returned to the subject troubling her. "But I don't know how much longer I can keep the will from Storm."

"Give me a week, Sarah. I need more time."

Sarah agreed.

"Little Bird," began Sarah a few days later at breakfast, "why do you appear fearful whenever I speak of the baby's birth?"

Little Bird tensed, pushing her unfinished breakfast plate away.

"There, you're doing it now!"

"She's afraid of childbirth," Dawn said, coming to the table and pouring herself coffee. "Her own mother died having her and Black Feather; they were twins."

The mother-to-be's eyes reflected unadulterated fear.

Sarah took Little Bird's hand. "Is that true, are you frightened of childbirth?" she asked tenderly.

Little Bird, teary eyed, nodded.

"Dawn and I are here and will do everything possible to see that nothing happens to you or the baby. If it will make you feel better, perhaps we could find a doctor." Sarah looked at Dawn hesitantly.

Dawn shook her head. "The nearest one is twenty miles away and refuses to treat Indians."

"Why?" Sarah asked indignantly.

Dawn hesitated. "His family was killed by Indians fifteen or twenty years ago."

"I guess that would explain why."

Little Bird spoke for the first time. "You must do something for me." She looked at Sarah pleadingly. "Black Feather promised to bring someone to help birth baby. Now that crew searches for Black Feather, he can't bring Comanche midwife. Take Little Bird to meet Black Feather. He promise to bring midwife to meeting place. If I have this woman, I will not be afraid."

Sarah and Dawn exchanged looks. "I don't know, Little Bird. I'm being guarded from Black Feather. He hasn't been exactly friendly to me."

"That is because I not yet tell him you are friend. I will do this if you go with me."

"Why haven't you told him?" Sarah asked.

"Wasn't sure if friendship was real. If you go with Little Bird, I will know you're friend for sure."

"Why do you need me along? You've been meeting your brother alone for weeks."

Little Bird blinked blankly at Sarah—the only sign of surprise that her trips had been noticed.

"I want brother to see you are friend and feel scared baby might come. Must not be alone anymore till baby come."

"What do you think, Dawn?" Sarah asked, searching Storm's mother's face for an inkling of her thoughts.

"I think you should ask Storm."

"No!" cried Little Bird, with flashing eyes. "Storm will harm Black Feather! Do not tell him!"

Sarah eyed the Indian girl carefully. "But Storm is your future husband. You wouldn't want to disobey him. He must come before your brother, if you truly love him."

Apparently confused, Little Bird hesitated.

"You *do* love Storm, don't you?" prodded Sarah.

"Black Feather is my twin brother," Little Bird murmured slowly.

"And Storm is your future husband," added Sarah.

"You don't have to fish for your answer, Sarah," Dawn proclaimed loudly. "Little Bird feels no love for my son. Do you, Little Bird? She just wants to be mistress of the ranch, with a white man's name for her baby."

At Sarah's startled look, Dawn added, "Not that she hasn't

a right to them, under the circumstances—just that love is not the reason she marries my son."

"Is that true, Little Bird?" Sarah asked gently.

"Yes," she answered, putting her chin up proudly.

Sarah took her hand again, "But Little Bird, wouldn't you rather marry for love, even if it meant living in a hut without a white man's name for your baby?"

"But Black Feather said. . . ," Little Bird slapped a hand over her own mouth.

"What did Black Feather say?" Sarah and Dawn chimed at once.

"Not important. About midwife—will you go with friend or not?"

Dawn stood. "*I'll* go with you."

"No," cried Little Bird. "I want Black Feather to see Sarah is friend."

"All right then, the three of us will go," suggested Dawn.

Again Little Bird protested. "No. Black Feather must see Sarah come alone with me. It shows true friendship to risk life for friend. It proves Little Bird is Sarah's friend."

"I'll go with you, Little Bird," Sarah said resolutely, glancing swiftly at Snakebite, lounging idly in the hall outside the dining room, unaware of their dangerous conversation. Sarah added softly, "I'll go, because you're my friend."

"And you will not tell Storm?" she asked anxiously.

"No."

"You?" she asked Dawn.

"I won't tell Storm—unless you aren't back within a reasonable timespan."

"When are we to meet Black Feather?" asked Sarah.

"Tomorrow at noon," answered Little Bird.

Sarah thought there was nothing more beautiful than a Texas sunset. Every evening she sat on the front porch steps, watching the red, yellow, and orange colored sky seem to slip behind the distant purple mountains. Sarah couldn't recall a sunset to compare, back in Chicago.

Would she remember everything about the ranch and Texas? How she dreaded going back! And would she be able to forget Storm? What about Aunt Emily? Naturally she'd want to stay with her husband, whom Sarah couldn't picture in a Chicago drawing room. These things passed between Sarah and the panoramic sunset. So engrossed was she that she failed to notice someone had settled beside her on the porch step.

"Do they have sunsets like this in Chicago?"

Sarah jumped at his voice. "Storm!" Then her eyes fed hungrily on him. How glad she was for his company that seemed so scarce these days. "I suppose," she answered, "Chicago must have sunsets like these, but I can't recall ever seeing them."

He stared ahead at the sunset. "Farthest north I've ever been was to college in Kansas City." He glanced at her, "What were you thinking about when I sat down? You seemed so deep in thought."

"I was memorizing everything—for future use."

"You're not thinking of leaving?" The sharp edge to his voice cut sharply through the evening silence.

"Did you think I'd stay and become your second wife, Indian style?" she flung bitterly.

He stared ahead in painful silence.

Sarah's voice softened. "I can't bear watching you ruin your life, Little Bird's, and mine. It's time I checked out. It's not going to be easy, leaving all this—and probably Aunt Emily, too!"

"You can't leave your own ranch, Sarah," he reminded, gently.

"But. . . ," she caught herself quickly, remembering her promise to Dawn. She'd have to wait a week or so, then give him the will and leave. "But. . . ," she quickly searched her mind for something else to fill in the sentence she'd started. "But . . . the baby. It should be here soon."

"I already spoke to Little Bird about that. I made her see that I can't marry her until the will is found, even if it means marrying after the baby comes. She put up a fuss, but I assured her it shouldn't be much longer."

"Giving us more time?" she asked. "But for what?"

"God is trying to show me something; I'm sure of it. But I can't tell what. Because of my emotional involvement, it's hard to tell whether God is speaking or my own heart. Often we think He is encouraging us in something we want, when in reality it's our own desire urging us.

"It's hard for me to believe, Sarah, that God would want me to go back on my word. He teaches us to live by truth and goodness, yet. . . ," he faltered.

"Yet what?" she prodded anxiously.

"Yet you were right about Little Bird. I don't think I've reached her with the Word of God. She goes to the services, but her life doesn't show her love and obedience to God. Then you enter my life: fresh, vibrant, and truthful. You accept God, you accept me and my people. Since the day I explained how to belong to God, the commitment has been evident in your life. Even your love for Little Bird is apparent." He shook his head. "I'm so confused, Sarah. How could God want me to neglect my responsibility to Little Bird and at the same time send me you?"

"But you're a preacher. You studied God's Word. Don't you know why? Your question sounds like one someone might ask you."

He shook his head, "I guess I'd tell anyone who asked that question to keep praying, that God will clarify his message and direction."

Sarah put her hand over his. "Then that is exactly what we'll do, preacher!"

He took her hand in both of his and raised it to his lips.

"You're good for me, Sarah," he whispered. Standing, he squeezed her hand then disappeared into the darkness.

Sarah's heart felt full and empty all at once.

She stood to go into the house and was startled to see Little Bird, huddling within the darkest corner of the porch.

"Little Bird, you startled me! Were you getting air, too?"

The swollen form came out from the shadows. "You love Storm?"

Sarah laughed nervously. "Me? I-I think Storm is—is a wonderful man. We're very good friends."

"Too bad," Little Bird said. "You could be Storm's second wife. We be close sisters."

"That's no longer allowed. God wants a man to have just one wife. The white man has been living by that rule for many years, and it seems to be the best way. But I'd like being a sister to you." Sarah put her arm around the Indian girl. "I'd like that very much."

Little Bird flinched at Sarah's affection. "You really like Little Bird? Would like her for sister?" Her face displayed pure bewilderment.

"Do I like Little Bird? No, I *love* Little Bird." Sarah leaned close to the Indian girl and kissed her forehead before marching into the house, leaving a puzzled Little Bird to stare at her back in wonder.

Early the next morning Sarah prepared for her journey with Little Bird. Dawn entered from the adjoining bedroom, with coffee. Sarah gave her a curious look.

"I didn't want to use the hall door and rouse Snakebite," she explained.

Sarah clapped her hands to her mouth. "Snakebite!" Her blue eyes searched the serene Dawn's for help. "How can I get away from him long enough to go with Little Bird?"

"I asked our little mother-to-be that very same question this morning, and she has promised to take care of it. I don't

know how, but I think this once we should ask no questions."
Dawn reached for Sarah's hands.

"I don't like this, Sarah. I'm glad you're helping Little Bird, but I don't like keeping it from Storm or having Little Bird hinder Storm's orders that Snakebite guard you. I also am worried about you."

"I feel uneasy, too. I prayed hard and long about it. But it's the only way I can prove my friendship, and if I can also make friends with Black Feather, I won't even need a guard any longer."

True to her word, when Sarah left her room, Snakebite was nowhere in sight.

Around eleven, Sarah and Little Bird slipped out the back door, scurrying for the woods nearby. Little Bird knew the way, through paths and shortcuts, and led Sarah at a swift, steady pace. Sarah tried to slow Little Bird, because of her condition, but Little Bird insisted on walking fast.

The Indian girl seemed quiet and tense, which confused Sarah, who'd thought Little Bird would be delighted with her company. Wasn't she proving her friendship? Perhaps it was Little Bird's pregnancy that made her moody.

Just before they reached the arranged place, Little Bird slowed. She looked at Sarah oddly. "It is just ahead."

"Are you all right? Do you want to rest?" asked Sarah.

"Why do you care about me?" Little Bird snapped angrily. Her eyes bored through Sarah, then moved beyond her and changed to recognition. Little Bird smiled warmly, joy aglow on her face.

Before Sarah could turn, she was grabbed from behind. Someone had one hand over her mouth, the other around her waist. Judging by the strength of the grasp, she knew struggling would be useless.

∼ 10 ∼

When Sarah made no move to free herself, the strong hand slipped from her mouth.

"White lady have no fire!" the voice from behind spat.

But Sarah stared ahead at Little Bird, who avoided Sarah's eyes.

"Why you no fight, white lady?" asked Black Feather bitterly. "Take the fun out of capture!"

Sarah continued staring into Little Bird's quick, darting eyes, but inwardly she prayed. Finally, having gathered strength from God, she said, "I'm not afraid, Black Feather. You can't do anything to me that my Father won't allow you to do."

"I see no father here," he growled, yanking her wrists behind her back with a coarse rope, tying them painfully.

"My Father, God. He's here and everywhere," she spoke calmly.

"You think your God can save you from Black Feather?" he barked.

"He will if He chooses."

"I not believe in your God, so He not harm Black Feather."

Sarah's eyes still begged for eye contact with Little Bird.

"Why do you do this, Little Bird? Storm won't marry you when he finds out."

Little Bird's frightened eyes flew to Black Feather for reassurance.

"Ha!" laughed Black Feather. "Storm never guess Little Bird in on this."

"You're wrong. His mother knows where I am and with whom," Sarah added.

Again Little Bird's doubting eyes flew to her twin brother.

"We make what happen to you look like accident. Little Bird will run to Storm, report you fall in creek and drown. He will believe Little Bird; he believe everything she tell him so far." He laughed hawkishly.

Little Bird glanced anxiously from her brother to Sarah, then started to speak, but instead winced, clutching her stomach. Black Feather hadn't caught the action, but Sarah had.

"What is it, Little Bird?" she asked anxiously.

The Indian girl straightened. "Why do you worry about me? Should be worrying about *self!*" she screamed, before again doubling in pain.

"The baby! It's the baby, isn't it, Little Bird?"

She nodded, tears streaming down her petrified face.

Black Feather rushed to his sister. Sarah tried moving her arms, but they were securely tied. She watched Black Feather carefully ease his sister to the ground. Yanking Sarah's shawl from her shoulders, he gently placed it beneath Little Bird's head.

"Not now, Little Bird—" he cried.

"Little Bird can't stop nature," replied Sarah, "but if you'll untie me, I'll help deliver the baby! I've seen it done."

"Free her!" gasped Little Bird.

"She get away, if I untie," said Black Feather, frowning.

"Let her go! See, brother, only her hands are tied. You didn't tie feet, and she not run. Loose her—make her help me!" Little Bird growled between clenched teeth.

Black Feather confronted Sarah. "You help my sister?"

Sarah nodded. "I didn't run because I *want* to help." She added softly, "Without my help, she could—" Little Bird's scream cut off Sarah's words.

Racing toward Sarah with knife unsheathed, Black Feather sliced the ropes, freeing her bound hands. She ran to Little Bird but spoke over her shoulder to the brother, "I need water. Can you bring me water in something?"

Black Feather looked around for a vessel to hold the water. There was nothing. Sarah noticed his knee-high buckskin boots. "Use your boots. Build a fire to warm the water."

In the meantime Sarah examined Little Bird as she'd seen old Doc Hudson do when her mother gave birth to her sister Luella. Sarah wouldn't think about Luella's having been stillborn; she'd only recall what Doc Hudson had done during the delivery.

According to what Sarah could feel, the baby was coming head first. She could foresee no problems, except calming Little Bird, who stiffened in terror.

"Little Bird, you must relax," Sarah scolded. "Relax, or the baby won't come."

Still Little Bird clenched her stomach in fear with each pain.

Sarah tried to remember how Doc had calmed her mother, though her mother hadn't thrashed and tensed like this Indian girl.

"Little Bird, breathe deeply. Hold it. Now let it out slowly." But Little Bird gritted her teeth and tightened her muscles against nature.

Black Feather returned, carrying his boots that overflowed with water. Sarah instructed him to place the boots as near the fire as possible without burning them. Then she turned to her patient again.

For several hours Sarah knelt on the ground, pleading, begging, cajoling Little Bird to relax and breathe deeply. Finally Little Bird obeyed, and the tiny, red, wrinkled body slid into Sarah's waiting hands. "Knife! I need the knife, Black Feather!"

As she remembered seeing Doc do, she cut the cord, placing the baby on the mother's stomach. Sarah handed the knife back to Black Feather.

"It's a little girl! What will you name her?" Sarah announced as the baby cried out hoarsely, thrashing her limbs wildly.

"A girl?" Little Bird asked groggily. "Not boy, like father?"

"No," Sarah corrected, "girl, like mother."

"Girl, like mother," repeated the proud mother. "Tiny Bird. She is Little Bird's, but smaller. She Tiny Bird," but Little Bird added quickly, "until she get white man's name!"

"Here," Sarah said, wrapping Tiny Bird in her shawl, "so she doesn't catch a cold."

Black Feather stood watching, his eyes full of awe. "What we do now?" he asked. "I drown lady that save sister and baby?"

Little Bird's eyes met Sarah's and narrowed beneath knitted brows. "You spoil plans. You make Storm sorry he make promise to Little Bird."

"I'm sorry. But why kill me? I'm going back to Chicago."

"You would do that for Little Bird?"

"I was preparing to leave anyway. I—"

Pounding hooves broke off her explanation. "That will be Storm." Sarah exhaled in relief.

"You will tell him?" asked Little Bird anxiously.

"No, but we'll talk more about this later."

Storm and several of the crew reined in wild, hard-ridden horses.

"Goodness," said Sarah, "you'd think Indians were chasing you!"

"What's going on?" thundered Storm. "Mother is frantic. She told me where you'd gone. What took so long? Why didn't you return?" His eyes darted swiftly from face to face, freezing dangerously on Black Feather. "Has he harmed you?"

"One question at a time," laughed Sarah. "First, meet Tiny Bird."

"So that's why you were detained," he said, glancing briefly at Little Bird and the baby. His relieved eyes returned to Sarah. "I'm glad you're all right."

Storm then spun around angrily to confront Black Feather, but he was gone.

Storm and the crew made a stretcher from branches, covering it with horse blankets upon which they laid the mother and baby, then attached it to Storm's horse. As Storm rode, Little Bird was gently dragged upon her bed.

For Sarah, the hardest job that day was riding in front of Storm. His arm held her waist tightly, scorching her like a branding iron, or so it felt. She did not tease, but rode sedately, praying they would reach the ranch before she softened under his touch and snuggled lovingly against his chest. It had been so long since she'd been close to him, and after what had happened that day, she needed comfort. The ride seemed endless, because they were forced to move slowly, pulling mother and child.

When they finally came into view of the house, Dawn stopped pacing the front porch and scampered down the drive to meet them. She helped Sarah dismount, hugging her affectionately before spotting Little Bird and her baby.

Cooing lovingly at the tiny bundle, Dawn took charge immediately, ordering the stretcher into the house and leading the entourage to Little Bird's room. Storm and Sarah found themselves awkwardly alone, watching everyone disappear into the house.

"Sure you're all right?" Storm's eyes scanned Sarah from head to toe.

Sarah nodded wearily.

"You did a wonderful thing today. Little Bird and her baby might have died out there without your help."

"It wasn't wonderful—just necessary." Sarah bit her lip. "Storm, I'm tired and dirty, but tomorrow I need to talk to you. Will you meet me in the study after breakfast?"

He agreed.

She ambled blindly to her room.

In the morning Sarah took her coffee into the study, where she found Storm at his desk, reclining comfortably in his chair. Sarah chose a chair near him, gracefully balancing her coffee cup on one knee.

"Have you been waiting long?"

"About an hour. But don't apologize, you needed the rest after yesterday."

"I can't remember ever being so tired," she said, appreciative of the concern in his smoky gray eyes.

After several moments of silence, Sarah cleared her throat, "Storm, I haven't been honest with you. I've purposely deceived you." She set her coffee cup on the desk and folded her hands in her lap.

He said nothing.

"A few weeks ago I discovered that I'm not Wilson's granddaughter. Not related to him or you, I've no claim on this ranch, yet I kept this information from you." She looked down at her hands nervously.

After an unbearable silence, Storm spoke. She strained to hear his almost-whispered words.

"My father told me the whole story. Still, he left the ranch to you in the first will—the only one found—therefore you are still the legal owner. Whether you're related to him or not, your name appears on the only will available."

"But that isn't all I've done to deceive you." She bent and pulled the paper from under the desk leg. "I found the second will and never told you." She handed the folded paper to him, shamefaced.

With one raised eyebrow, he unfolded the paper, scanned it briefly, then handed it back. "You are mistaken, Sarah. This is nothing but an old bunkhouse duty roster."

Sarah grabbed the paper and examined it with disbelief. "But it was here. I saw it!"

Storm leaned back in his chair and smiled, his gray eyes twinkling mischievously. "The day you hurt your head?"

"No!" She bent to remove the paper wad from the other desk leg, but found only the newspaper page. "Your mother was with me when I found it." Sarah scurried to the door, "Wait right here." She went out and returned moments later, dragging a reluctant Dawn.

"Dawn, tell Storm what we found that day under the desk leg," commanded Sarah.

With a mixture of guilt and confusion on her face, Dawn looked from Sarah to Storm. "I don't know what you're talking about, Sarah. Perhaps you need more rest. Yesterday was—"

"I'm fine," Sarah cut in. "Tell him the truth, Dawn. I can no longer live this horrid lie. It's time for me to set things straight and . . . and leave."

"You can't leave!" Storm protested, sitting upright. "The ranch legally belongs to you."

Sarah's eyes darted from Dawn to Storm before comprehension struck her. "I know what you two are up to, and I love you both for it, but it won't work." Close to tears, she cried, "I have to leave. Don't you see?" She closed her eyes to better compose herself.

"Storm," she continued, "you have a responsibility toward Little Bird. I understand that, even accept it. But I can't stay here and be part of it. If you both care, just let me go!"

Storm rose and placed his hands on Sarah's shoulders. "Have you lost your faith?" he asked softly. "We just need more time." He donned his wide-brimmed hat, "Keep praying, Sarah." He quietly left the room.

Sarah sighed and glanced at Dawn, who was also preparing to quietly exit. "Oh, no you don't. You come back!"

Dawn reluctantly turned back to face Sarah.

"You either told Storm about the will or he knew the whole time! What did the two of you do with the will? Hide it?"

Eyes downcast, Dawn said, "I'm sorry, Sarah. I can tell you nothing. But if I did anything to displease you, it's because I love you both."

Sarah sighed helplessly, "I must leave Arrow C."

Biting her lip with a worried frown, Dawn said, "Do as Storm advised. Wait and pray."

The following afternoon Sarah paid Little Bird and her baby a visit. The new mother lay in bed, her daughter bundled beside her. The beautiful Indian girl smiled when Sarah entered. "I tell Tiny Bird all about you."

Sarah smiled serenely, looking down on the sleeping baby.

"She needs white man's name. *Sarah* good name. You will let Tiny Bird use that name?"

"Yes. At least there will be a Sarah here at Arrow C for a long time, but just one." At Little Bird's puzzled look Sarah added, "I must return to Chicago."

"You make friends with Little Bird, save mine and my daughter's life—and now go?" Little Bird asked.

Sarah nodded. "It's best this way. You'll be getting married, and I'll be in the way. You and Storm deserve to be alone with your family."

"Sit!" demanded Little Bird, pointing to a chair beside her bed.

Sarah obeyed.

"You think I would let Black Feather kill you that day?"

"Would you have?"

"I planned with Black Feather to kill you, but did not want to when time came. I felt sad and scared here," Little Bird pointed to her stomach. "Little Bird think just before pain start, *How can I stop brother from killing friend?* Little Bird does something else, pray to Storm's God." She bowed her head with shame, "I never prayed before, only pretend, to make Storm happy. Little Bird prayed for way to stop Black Feather—that was when pains start." She smiled shyly at Sarah, "Storm is right, his God *does* love Little Bird." She kissed her daughter's head gently.

Sarah blinked her tearing eyes quickly. "It makes me happy to know you didn't want to kill me. It hurt very much knowing you wanted to drown me. Thank you for being my friend. Now I'll repay the favor and leave so that you can be happy with your family." Sarah stood and walked to the door. "Keep praying, Little Bird, and teach little Sarah how to pray, too."

After leaving Little Bird, Sarah felt depressed and decided to pay Aunt Emily a visit. She saddled Red and headed in that direction but decided to stop first at her quiet place. She'd missed her time there that morning, detained by Broken Wing, who had insisted Red needed shoeing.

Perhaps visiting her favorite place, followed by a quiet chat with Aunt Emily, would cheer her.

Approaching the brook at a slow trot, she was surprised to see Storm leaning over the bridge rail, deep in thought. He glanced her way and waved.

Sarah tied Red and joined him. "So this is when you visit our haven."

"It's the perfect place to think," he said. "Knowing you come here mornings, I visit later in the day."

"If you'd rather be alone, I'll leave. I was on my way to see Aunt Emily anyway."

"No. I've been here long enough. That fence awaits me."

"Storm, I was thinking about something. . . ."

He laughed. "Yes, I can see you have a question, Curious Eyes!"

"Will you answer it?" she asked earnestly.

He gazed at her sympathetically, "If I can."

"If you knew the whole time I wasn't Wilson's real

granddaughter, why did you make me think we were related?"

"Can't I have any secrets?"

"Not when they concern me."

Storm looked away. "I was trying to discourage you. I couldn't tell you the truth—it wasn't my secret to tell. But I knew it would be troublesome if you continued growing fond of me, as you so boldly confessed that day. You being the correctly reared young lady, I thought that our being related would surely end your frivolous romantic notions. Which is what I thought your feelings were—and with my promise to Little Bird. . . . I just thought it would unclutter things."

"I'm too low in spirit to even respond to your accusation that I had *romantic notions*. Romantic notions, indeed."

He put his arm around her lightly. "Why so sad? You aren't still planning to leave?"

She looked up into his eyes, putting her arms around his neck. "Storm, I can't stay. Meetings like this are inevitable and also forbidden." Tears escaped her eyes before she could control them.

Storm responded, lovingly, by gently pressing her golden head against his chest and stroking her long, silky hair as one would comfort a child.

"Outward displays of affection—definitely not a good idea for us now. But listen to my heart beating, Sarah? It aches for you. God is in that heart, too, and because of that, I know things will work out."

She listened to the steady thumping of his heart. God made that heart; God nurtured that heart; God loved that heart. God was in that heart. Would God want Storm to marry someone he didn't love, just because he gave his word?

Looking up at him through her tears, she smiled. "I want to keep praying, but I don't want my friend Little Bird hurt either. Would God want me to hurt her? Yet how can I have *you* without hurting *her*? And now, it's more than just coming between you and Little Bird, now I'm breaking up a *family!*"

"Sometimes things aren't as impossible as they seem," Storm consoled.

"What happened the other day in the woods with Little Bird and Black Feather?" Storm asked, stepping back to hold her at arm's length.

"I accompanied Little Bird to meet her brother. She wanted to see him and feared going alone. She said I would prove my friendship by going, on account of Black Feather's threats on my life. She promised to tell him we were friends. I thought it worth the danger to win Black Feather's trust, too, yet we hadn't met Black Feather but a few minutes when Little Bird's pains began. I did what anyone else would have done, delivered the baby."

He kissed her forehead. "Another woman might have been jealous and let her enemy die. Had you let Little Bird die. . . ."

Sarah reached out and covered Storm's lips with her hand. "The thought never entered my mind."

"Proving you're truly one of God's own."

"That's the nicest thing anyone has ever said to me."

"I love you, Sarah," he whispered, looking at her soul through her eyes.

"I've waited so long to hear you say those words," she choked. Quickly kissing his cheek, she dashed away to her horse.

That evening, Sarah sat on her usual porch step, watching another magnificent sunset. Storm joined her.

"I always know where to find you, come sundown," he laughed. "How was your visit with Emily?"

"I always enjoy my visits. She and Manny are so happy and have fixed up the cottage beautifully. Last weekend Manny built a fireplace for their parlor. Today Aunt Emily made yellow curtains for her kitchen window." Sarah sighed, "I don't think I've ever seen her so happy!"

"And you're so unhappy, is that what the sigh meant?"

"Why don't you admit you have the will and let me go home?" she countered.

"Is that what you really want?"

"What I want doesn't matter," she murmured softly. "I can't have what I want."

With a strong, clear voice, Storm said. "If it's God's will that we be together, we will be. But we have to give Him time to work things out through us."

"And," Sarah returned, "how much time will it take? I really feel I should leave. If things work out in our favor, I can always come back. The way things stand now, I feel like an intruder."

Sarah stood up and turned toward the house. Storm took her hand. "Don't go yet."

"The sunset has passed," she said. "I'm anxious to be alone and talk with God. I've so much to say tonight."

"Sit with me a few more minutes," he said, pulling her gently back down beside him.

He kept her hand in his. "You had a visitor today."

❧ *11* ❧

"*A* visitor? Who?" Sarah asked.

"Samuel Lewis," Storm said. "He came while you were visiting Emily."

"Why didn't you send for me?"

He shrugged. "He'll be back, you can bet on that."

"You don't like Mr. Lewis!"

"I like everyone."

"Then why have you suddenly turned glum and tense?"

"I like him, it's just that he—I mean his. . . . Well, maybe I *don't* like him."

"Storm! What could this man have done for you, of all people, to dislike him? He spoke highly of you in his letter to us."

"It's his patronizing attitude toward the Indians, I guess. I try to like him, God knows I do. I don't hate him, mind you. I just don't enjoy his company."

"Then I won't either," said Sarah supportively.

"Somehow, I think you will." He pulled his hand away. "Lewis has a way with women. Mother, Rosa, Little Bird—all dote on him."

"Why, Storm, you're jealous!" Sarah laughed.

He frowned. "Maybe, a little."

"And you think I'll be charmed by him?"

He studied her. "I don't know."

"Is that why you didn't send for me?"

"Partly. He wants you to sign some papers having to do with owning the ranch."

"And. . . ," she coaxed.

"And I just thought it too early to be signing papers."

"Because you aren't ready to show the second will?" she asked.

"You still think I have it?" His face, illuminated by moonlight, appeared amused.

"I know you have it. I'm just not sure what you plan to do with it and when."

Storm merely smiled.

"I wondered about something else today," Sarah continued. "You said you were close to your father. If this is true, why doesn't his fatherhood out of wedlock disgust you? Surely you, a man of God, don't approve?"

"It did disgust me at first. But you have to understand the situation. My mother, believe it or not, practically pushed him into this dilemma. It raged as a family sore spot for years. My father worshiped my mother. His first wife, your grandmother, he never loved—it was a marriage of convenience. When she died, he met and fell in love with my mother. The wedding ceremony was Comanche, not binding by white man's law.

"They were happy. When my mother complained about being the only wife—can you imagine that?—my father became furious with her. He thought he flattered her by saying he wanted no other but her. Instead he discovered he had insulted her. The battle raged for years, but that's not the worst. My mother brought other women to the ranch and practically threw them at him! Little Bird was her last attempt at matchmaking. Evidently, he gave in, tired of fighting. What we can't figure out is why he never told us about it.

139

Even on his deathbed he said nothing. Mother thinks it's because he didn't understand Indian ways and because of his upbringing must have thought his marriage to Little Bird should be kept secret."

"Then he *did* marry Little Bird?" Sarah asked, surprised.

"Little Bird claims they went through a small ceremony among a few Comanche—Black Feather and his friends."

"So you've forgiven them?"

He nodded. "And thought it my duty to take care of the girl and her baby, since it was my parents' fault this all happened."

"I see. Well," she said standing, "next time Samuel Lewis comes, be sure to call me. I have questions for him, too."

"You won't sign anything?" Storm asked anxiously, walking her to the front door.

"I won't sign anything."

Storm kissed her hands. "Good night, Sarah. Sleep well."

Though warned of Lewis's probable return, Sarah was surprised the next day when Dawn announced her visitor.

Stepping out of her room, Sarah glanced over the balcony. There stood one of the handsomest men she'd ever seen. At that moment he glanced up and their eyes locked. He appeared younger than Sarah had pictured him and more sophisticated looking. For some reason Sarah had envisioned him as a man of her grandfather's age, not this tall, handsome young man in his early thirties.

Mr. Lewis's eyes followed her as she descended the stairs. He stood tall, taller than Storm, who towered over her. But unlike Storm, he wore his light hair short, and he constantly petted a thin, straight mustache.

"Allow me to introduce myself," he said cordially. "I'm Samuel Lewis, your grandfather's attorney, and yours also if you so wish." He reached for her hand and kissed it, then relinquished it somewhat reluctantly.

"Please be seated, Mr. Lewis." Sarah sat on a wing chair

near the sofa he chose. "Your business in Fort Worth went well, I hope?" Samuel Lewis, she noted, certainly appeared handsome and debonair but had the look of one who seldom ventured outdoors. His perfect features, while attractive, were in direct contrast to Storm's rugged, muscular appearance.

"Very well, thank you. And your journey?" he countered, still smoothing his mustache.

"Extremely rough from Chicago to Dodge City. From Dodge to Arrow C the traveling was most enjoyable. Storm did a remarkable job."

"Storm! Yes, a good man," he said, adding offhandedly, "almost white."

"Almost white?" Sarah gasped, wondering what he meant by that.

"An expression meaning he is almost on *our* level."

"Almost? *Our* level?"

"Of course you know he's half Indian. We, that is, the entire community, rank him as Indian."

Sarah protested, "What difference does it make?"

"If your family had been massacred by Indians, would a half-breed look any better to you?" he asked with a knowing smile.

Sarah thought his smile the phoniest she'd ever seen. She disliked Samuel Lewis, his smile, his attitude, and his much fondled mustache.

"I'll warn you Mr. Lewis, I've become close friends with the Indians here and won't hear talk against them."

Mr. Lewis shook his head. "Friends? You aren't serious? Why, the other ranchers and myself thought you'd be different, coming from Chicago and all. We hoped Arrow C would finally be white, like the other ranches in the area. If we'd have known. . . ." He shook his head frowning. "So you'll follow in your grandfather's footsteps and continue to indulge these savages."

"They do a good job, why not?"

"Why not? Look here, our families—"

"Mr. Lewis," Sarah interrupted, deciding it best to change the subject, "are you aware of the possibility of a second will?"

"There is only one will, and it names you as heir."

"You're sure?"

"I would know, being Wilson's lawyer."

"Or would you destroy your copy of a second will if the beneficiary were an Indian?"

Lewis stood abruptly. "Miss Clarke, are you accusing me of something?" he asked with angry indignation.

"I'm only asking, Mr. Lewis. You're extremely defensive for someone who isn't guilty."

Samuel Lewis scooped up his papers. "And I had thought we'd get along famously. If you'll just sign these two papers, I'll be on my way."

Sarah rose and glared up at the tall man defiantly. "I won't sign anything today."

"But you must! It's just formality. These papers simply show you've accepted your inheritance and are the rightful owner stated in the will." Samuel Lewis mopped his face with his handkerchief. "Please, Miss Clarke, it's hot, I'm tired, and I'm angry—having been insulted in your home. Sign the papers, and I won't bother you again."

"I'm sorry if I've offended you, Mr. Lewis, but I only asked a few simple questions. You had only to answer them. There was no need to become insulted or angry. Have I no right to ask questions?"

Samuel Lewis shook his head and sighed. "Let me apologize then, for it's hot and I'm travel worn. I've been on the road for days. When I missed you yesterday, I spent the night at the nearest neighboring ranch, the Wade's. I'm anxious to get to my own home. But I have to settle this business first. To lose my temper with such a lovely woman is totally unlike me. Will you forgive me, my dear?"

"Of course." Sarah steadied herself. She was falling for his charm, too! She decided to give the man another chance but also to be very careful of his charming manipulation.

"Where are my manners? Let's sit out on the porch. I'll have Rosa bring us some cool lemonade." Sarah opened the kitchen door and gave Rosa the order before escorting Mr. Lewis to the porch.

A slight breeze made it cooler on the porch, and Samuel Lewis smiled in appreciation when Rosa brought the lemonade. Although old enough to be Lewis's mother, Rosa blushed and giggled with downcast eyes while he flirted with her. *Storm was right*, Sarah thought. *Women do like Samuel Lewis.*

"Do you feel better, Mr. Lewis?" she asked after Rosa disappeared.

"Yes, much, thank you. Your beauty throws me off balance, and I keep forgetting why I'm here. The papers," he spread them out before her, smiled, and winked, "if you'll just sign here and here."

Sarah shook her head. "I'm sorry, not today."

Lewis reddened. "I don't understand. No one has ever refused to sign inheritance papers!"

"I didn't say I wouldn't sign them. I said, 'Not today.' "

"You're stubborn, like your grandfather!"

"That's odd, because Wilson wasn't my grandfather," Sarah blurted in anger, then realized she should have waited until he'd finished sipping his lemonade, for now he was choking.

"Are you all right, Mr. Lewis?"

"Yes, yes." He coughed. "I'll be all right. Did you say Wilson wasn't your grandfather?"

"That's right. I found my grandmother's diary in the attic. She was a widow with child when she married Wilson Clarke. That child was my father."

Lewis looked uncomfortable. "Who else knows of this?"

"My aunt, Dawn, and Storm."

"You told Storm?"

"Why does that bother you?" She studied him carefully.

"He'll try to get the ranch from you! Why did you tell him? Don't you know he'd do *anything* to get this ranch? I wouldn't be surprised if he planted the diary—or tried to forge a will. I never trust a back-stabbing Indian—"

Sarah stood, and spoke carefully. "I warned you, Mr. Lewis. I won't have Storm or the others criticized, especially in that manner. Storm is the finest man I've ever met. He wouldn't think of doing the things you suggested. In fact, he knew I wasn't Wilson's granddaughter the whole time and never tried to use it against me.

"I think you had better leave, Mr. Lewis. You won't get your papers signed, because I'm not keeping the ranch. I intend to sign it over to Storm. Draw up papers of that nature, and I'll sign them!"

Dawn entered then and Samuel's anger disappeared and he was the master of charm once again. He flirted and flattered Dawn until she looked as Rosa had moments earlier, like a smitten young schoolgirl. Sarah noticed his slick mannerisms and honeyed words. *This man has his act down pat*, she thought.

"Sorry I didn't welcome you sooner, but I was helping Little Bird bathe her baby," Dawn explained, blushing.

"Little Bird had her baby?" he asked.

"Yes, a daughter. In fact, she wants me to bring you up to see her and the baby."

"I'd love to." He followed Dawn into the house and up the stairs.

Relieved, Sarah fled to the stables, saddled and mounted Red, and galloped to her quiet place.

Amid the babbling of the brook, Sarah calmed herself of the hostile feelings brought on by Mr. Lewis. She cringed, remembering the things the man had said. How dare he attack Storm! Why Storm was ten times the man Mr. Lewis was or could ever hope to be. Why couldn't Rosa, Dawn, and Little Bird see him as she did?

The brook sparkled and gurgled, the birds sang, and Sarah

began to feel the calming effect. How this place could soothe her! Even Mr. Lewis couldn't spoil—

The sound of hoofbeats broke into Sarah's thoughts. Her heart pounded. Storm! Afternoons he came here for his quiet time. She smiled. He always managed to appear just when she needed him most! She anticipated running into his arms to be comforted and soothed from her unpleasant encounter. The figure dismounted and walked toward the bridge. Sarah noticed the stiff, arrogant gait and felt disappointment surge through her. It wasn't Storm.

The tall, thin man strode to the base of the bridge, hat in hand. The thin lips beneath the sly mustache smiled. "May I join you?"

How had Samuel Lewis found her and for what purpose? She'd thought her insults had sent him off Arrow C for good.

"At your own risk, Mr. Lewis," she replied coldly.

He approached cautiously. "I've come waving a white flag. I'm calling a truce. Please cease firing."

With arms akimbo, she replied, "I'll stop firing when you stop insulting my friends."

He held up his right hand, "I promise."

"Very well." She leaned over the bridge rail. "Why did you follow me? What do you want? I meant what I said. I won't sign anything today."

"I've come to beg you not to do anything foolish with the ranch just yet." He leaned against the railing and gazed down at the trickling, swirling brook. "This is a lovely spot. Do you come here often?"

She nodded, wondering what his next move would be.

"I can see why. It's lovely—as you are! I've been looking forward to our meeting, Miss Clarke, but now wish I'd waited until I was well rested and less irritable. I'm afraid we've gotten off to a bad start." He smiled flirtatiously. "Let's begin again."

Sarah studied him. What could he possibly want from her? Would he go to this much trouble for her signature on a few papers? Though she'd been rude, he crawled back for more. She'd made it clear she didn't want to hear insults about her friends, but what seemed to rile him most was her intention to sign the ranch over to an Indian. Was he now trying to initiate a friendship so he could talk her out of it? Or as it were, "charm" her out of it? Was Storm's owning the ranch such a threat to the community? Was it merely friendship this man was trying to develop with her—or something more?

Sarah spoke cautiously, "I select my friends very carefully."

"I know. That's why I'd be fortunate to be considered one."

"The Indians weren't my friends at first, but they proved their worthiness in almost no time at all." Sarah measured him thoughtfully. "And if you're proposing something more than friendship, I'm not interested."

"You're very frank, aren't you?" He laughed, fingering his mustache nervously.

"If being frank is the same as being honest, yes."

"I think honesty is a bit more subtle," he chuckled. "Usually blunt people, such as yourself, appreciate the trait in others, so I'll be open with you. I'm interested in becoming *very* close friends. I find your frankness amusing, your opinions interesting, and your personality refreshing." He put out his hand to touch her hair. "To say nothing of your loveliness."

Sarah heard his honeyed words, observed his obliging smile, but noticed that somewhere in between, his eyes remained detached.

She stepped back from his hand and smiled indulgently. "What is it you *really* want, Mr. Lewis?"

"How can we be friends if you call me Mr. Lewis? My friends call me Sam." He raised his eyebrows dramatically. "May I call you Sarah?"

"You may, if you stop insulting my friends."

"Very well, Sarah." He moved closer and whispered, "A lovely name for a lovely lady."

Sarah had the urge to laugh. Did he really think she'd fall for his phony lines?

He continued, "I'd like you to accompany me on calls to neighboring ranches. They're most eager to meet you. Say, tomorrow?"

"None have made an effort to meet me, but if you're certain they are anxious, what time should we be ready?"

"We?"

"Yes, Storm, Dawn, and myself."

"Oh, I had a more intimate traveling party in mind. Like just you and I."

"I'm afraid that's impossible." Sarah studied him. It wasn't disappointment evident on his face, but frustration.

Suddenly Lewis grabbed her shoulders and bent close with lips puckered. She leaned away from him until she thought her back would snap. "What are you doing?" she cried. "Stop, at once!"

"Look Sarah, I'm attracted to you, so let's not waste time on amenities. I think I've fallen in love with you. I find you irresistible. Come here," he grabbed for her again, smearing his thin, dry lips over her face, trying to target her lips, which Sarah managed to move back and forth too swiftly for him to hit.

Sarah's back hurt from arching away from his awkward embrace, and her neck ached from pivoting her face away from his determined lips. If it weren't so painful, she'd laugh over the spectacle they must have made.

Both froze at the sound of a man's loud, angry voice. "I think, Mr. Lewis, you've finally worn out your welcome."

Continuing his assault on Sarah, Lewis laughed, then sneered, "Not now, Injun boy, can't you see I'm busy?"

Scowling, Storm dismounted and stood, hands on hips, a few feet away. "Take your hands off Miss Clarke!"

Lewis gripped Sarah's shoulders painfully. "It isn't Miss

147

Forbidden Legacy

Clarke anymore, it's Sarah. And it isn't any of your business. Go build a teepee, do a rain dance, or whatever you Indians do."

Between clenched teeth Storm warned, "This Indian will do what Indians do best, if you don't unhand Miss Clarke. *Now!*" he added sharply.

Lewis dropped his hands.

"I think you'd better leave Arrow C, *Mr.* Lewis," Sarah said, rubbing the grip marks from her shoulders.

"I will, but only because I know he has about a dozen Indians hidden in the brush to assist him. Indians never attack alone; they're not brave enough for one-on-one combat."

Sarah watched Storm's eyes flash and his nostrils flare angrily, yet he made no further comment.

Lewis swaggered toward his horse. "You're a very foolish woman, Sarah."

"Miss Clarke," she corrected.

Sarah and Storm silently watched Mr. Lewis ride away. Storm crossed the bridge with several of his long strides and took Sarah into his arms. She laid her head against his chest tenderly.

"I was wrong," he said, stroking her hair lightly.

"Wrong?"

"You *didn't* like Mr. Lewis's company."

"He's a persuasive man but had no luck getting me to sign the papers, so he tried using charm. Poor Mr. Lewis! He had no way of knowing his charm would have no effect on a woman already hopelessly in love." She gazed up at him, stroking his cheek. "By the way, just what is it Indians do best?"

"Let me show you," he whispered, bringing his lips down gently on hers.

The next evening Sarah knocked softly on Dawn's bedroom door. At Dawn's welcome, Sarah entered cheerlessly.

"What's wrong, Sarah?"

"I haven't seen Storm all day. Do you know where he is?"

"Not exactly." Dawn patted Sarah's shoulder affectionately. "He's all right though, somewhere on the ranch."

"But he hasn't come in for meals, and Aunt Emily said he hasn't eaten with the men at the bunkhouse either," Sarah fretted.

"He may be praying and fasting. He does this once in a while when greatly troubled or burdened. I don't understand, but it always does him good. He seems to get the answers he needs, for afterwards he's always in a better mood."

"You're sure he's all right?" Sarah asked, her forehead still creased.

"It breaks a mother's heart to see the woman her son's not marrying so much in love with him. Come, sit down," she urged gently.

"Dawn," said Sarah hopefully, "you mentioned that you were working on something that might help Storm and me—"

"Oh, that," Dawn frowned. "It came to nothing. I'm sorry."

"May I ask what your plan was?"

"Hunter and I thought if we snooped and asked around at the reservation we'd hear something useful. Deep inside I still doubt Tiny Bird is Wilson's baby. I have for some time. I know it's foolish, but. . . ." She bit her lip nervously. "Anyway, we had a few leads, but no proof. Hunter discovered Little Bird had a few romances during the time in question. Two of the three questioned denied any intimacy. The third Hunter couldn't locate to question." Dawn shrugged. "We were wrong. Little Bird was a good Indian girl with a virtuous past."

Sarah patted Dawn's hand lovingly. "Thank you for trying."

*   *   *

When Sarah came down for breakfast the next morning, Dawn excitedly told her that Storm had called a meeting, ordering her, Sarah, Little Bird, Hunter, Aunt Emily, and Manny to be present in the study in one hour.

Questions raced through Sarah's mind as she breakfasted without knowing what she ate. Freshening herself quickly, she arrived in the study on time.

They were all sitting in chairs facing Storm's desk. Sarah, the last to enter, had just settled into a chair beside Manny when Storm entered the room. His eyes scanned the gathering as if counting and mentally checking each name on his list. He remained standing, leaning against the front of the old oak desk.

Typically Indian, he stood with arms folded across his chest. He cleared his throat. "Thank you for coming.

"I'd like to announce a decision I made last night, with God's help." He paused, glancing at every face, his eyes softening as they met Sarah's.

Storm's manner of urgency alarmed Sarah. Would his decision change their relationship? For better or worse?

"It's not Sunday, so I won't give a sermon. I'll just say briefly that God spoke to me last night, and I've been awakened." He scanned his audience. "I thought God was pulling me from both ends recently, my affairs seemed so muddled. I kept asking God, 'Why?' I couldn't understand Him. But I know now, it was me, not God, causing my difficulties. I promised to live according to His Word, but one of my human weaknesses got the better of me. Greed. I lusted after this ranch, even to the point of hurting others. I was obsessed with owning Arrow C above all else.

"Not that we shouldn't desire nice things or be ambitious to succeed materially—but it shouldn't be our main goal in life. And it shouldn't hurt others. Wanting the ranch has only brought heartache and misery. Therefore I'm publically conceding the ranch to its rightful owner, Sarah Clarke."

Sarah gasped in surprise.

"Of course," he continued, "I'll stay and work the ranch as long as she'll have me, for the same compensation as I receive now."

Pulling a folded paper from his pocket, Storm struck a match on his boot bottom, touched the flame to the paper, and threw it into the fireplace.

Sarah opened her mouth to protest, but Storm's warning look silenced her.

Emily and Manny exchanged baffled glances and shrugged. Dawn wiped her eyes with a handkerchief, sniffling loudly. Hunter grunted. Only Little Bird jumped up to protest.

"What about your promise?" she cried.

Storm spoke calmly, and gently. "I made the promise in good faith and will honor it."

"But Little Bird get no ranch? Not be house mistress? Where will Little Bird sleep? In bunkhouse with other cowboys?" She questioned furiously.

"I'm sorry, Little Bird. I promised you my name, security, and support, nothing more. I will, however, be a good, kind husband."

Little Bird glared at the occupants of the room bitterly before storming out, slamming the door behind her.

Storm stood with head bowed, humbly. "That's all, meeting adjourned."

Slowly everyone filed out except Sarah, who sat staring at the charred paper ashes in the hearth.

Unsure of Storm's new attitude, she didn't know what to say. Did his new resolution exclude her? She gathered her courage and blurted the question foremost on her mind. "The paper you burned—was it the second will?"

"Yes."

She shook her head, befuddled. "But why? It proved the ranch belonged to you."

"I thought I wanted it—I still do—but not at the expense of hurting others," he replied.

"How would claiming your rightful inheritance hurt others?"

"If you leave, everyone will be hurt. Dawn loves you dearly; she'll be hurt, to say nothing of Aunt Emily, Manny, and the whole crew. Even Rosa adores you. The community is bound to make trouble; Lewis will see to that. And last, even I would be hurt. I envisioned *my ranch* without you. I'd never have another happy moment, if you left Arrow C. This place is meaningless and worthless to me without you.

"But foremost, I truly believe that this is what God wants me to do, and I feel good about it, like stepping out of a bath, clean, leaving all dirt and grime behind."

Sarah gave Storm a bewildered look. "How will your giving me the ranch keep me here when you still plan to marry Little Bird? I cannot stay and watch you and Little Bird—"

"Trust me," Storm cut in. "I'm doing what I believe God wants me to do without questioning. What I've done today feels too right to be wrong. Trust God, Sarah. And if you can't trust Him, trust me, because if anyone has to leave this ranch, it will be me, not you. I promise."

~~ 12 ~~

Sarah watched the late afternoon shadows rob the study of its brightness. The house was too still. She wondered if everyone remained as stunned as she over Storm's announcement that morning.

She shook her head sadly, still unable to understand. Storm didn't want the ranch, it was hers. Why did she feel no joy over her triumph? He'd said his lust for the ranch hurt others, especially because it meant she would leave. Why did he think she would stay now? Just because the ranch was hers didn't mean she'd stay. How could she bear to stay when he married Little Bird? He had said, if anyone left, it would be him. Would he and Little Bird move out then?

Walking to the study window, she gazed out over the lawn behind the house. The grass that had been so green when she'd arrived had turned brown from the hot sun.

A sudden movement at the far corner of the house caught Sarah's eye. Little Bird and Storm appeared, walking slowly, talking animatedly.

Suddenly Sarah felt like an intruder. Had she any right to spy? Yet she became unable to move. *I'll only watch them for a moment*, she thought.

Storm and Little Bird walked toward the big cottonwood but no longer gestured wildly. Sarah concluded from their motions and facial expressions that they now conversed in soft tones. Little Bird seemed to be doing most of the talking, and the discussion appeared emotional and serious in nature.

Sarah, about to turn away, saw Storm encircle Little Bird within his arms and hold her tenderly. The Indian girl clung to him, weeping convulsively.

What did this mean? Did they love each other after all? Although it hurt to see Storm embracing another, Sarah couldn't command her feet away from the window.

She watched Storm wipe Little Bird's tears with his large bandana. Urging Little Bird to sit beneath the tree, he continued comforting her by holding her hand, patting it now and then as he spoke to her, with head bent close.

Forcing herself from the window, Sarah raced up the stairs and threw herself upon the bed and cried convulsively. Her cry was long overdue. Weeks of suppressed emotions flooded to the surface.

Thoroughly spent, she dried her eyes and propped herself into a sitting position. Though now battling a bout of hiccups from her emotional upheaval, she felt better. She had to analyze the situation and put things in proper perspective.

What did this mean? This morning Storm had forfeited his right to the ranch. Little Bird had been noticeably bitter over his decision. Had Storm smoothed things between them? Was this, then, the beginning of the end for her and Storm? But she'd known all along this moment was coming. Why cry over it now?

She dropped to her knees.

"Lord, like Storm, my life is Yours to do with as You will. Yet I'm human, and things hurt. Please settle this quickly between Storm, myself, and Little Bird. Is Storm the man you want me to spend my life with? Show me now, Lord, so I can deal with it and get on with life. Maybe Little Bird is Your choice for Storm; then help me continue without him. Should

I leave? Or ask them to leave? Guide me, Lord, for without You, I'll mess things up. I need Your expert guidance. Amen." Sarah felt a surge of courage ripple through her.

She undressed and washed from the pitcher and basin. Moving to the wardrobe, she selected a rose-colored silk with the new, smaller-style bustle, which she'd bought in Saint Louis and never worn. She chose it to wear tonight because Manny and Aunt Emily were celebrating one month of marriage with a housewarming party, and everyone on the ranch was invited to their cottage. Aunt Emily had suggested they dress in their stylish city clothes for old times' sake. Her aunt had stayed after Storm's speech and styled her hair.

She modeled before the mirror, feeling foreign in the tailored finery. The dress, while lovely, was as out of place here as her homespun would be in a Chicago drawing room. She sighed and supposed it wouldn't hurt to wear the clothes on special occasions, if only as a remembrance of her previous life.

Picking up a pink feather, she wove it into her hairdo. As a final touch, she pinched her cheeks, smiled at the reflection, and turned to go. She flung open the bedroom door and gasped to see a figure standing, ready to knock.

"Why, Little Bird," Sarah gasped in surprise. "Did you wish to see me?"

The Indian girl nodded, dropping the hand that had been poised to knock.

"Come in, sit here on the bed." Sarah sat beside her. "You've been crying. Is something wrong?"

Little Bird nodded again. Her large brown eyes stared longingly at Sarah's dress and hair. "Pretty," she whispered, reaching out to touch the fabric lightly.

"Would you like a dress like this?" Sarah asked, suddenly inspired with an idea.

Leaving Little Bird perched on the bed, she rummaged through the wardrobe until she found the perfect dress, a green satin with a large bustle of white lace ruffling down the back. She handed it to the awestricken Indian girl.

"For me?" Little Bird whispered.

Sarah nodded. "I'll help you put it on. That's what sisters are for, you know." Sarah smiled warmly.

To Sarah's surprise, Little Bird threw the dress aside and embraced her so hard, she nearly took Sarah's breath away.

Tears streamed down Little Bird's face. "First, let Little Bird say what came to say. Already talk with Storm. He say talk to you. I should have before but was afraid you be angry with Little Bird. Storm say truth always best, and you never angry with truth." The Indian girl hung her head shamefully. With big brown eyes peeking through lowered lashes, she spoke so softly Sarah had to strain to hear. "Little Bird lied. Little Sarah is not Wilson Clarke's baby. Poor man died, and Black Feather tell Little Bird to blame him, get ranch and lots of money. Wilson Clarke never even look at Little Bird. Little Sarah's father was bad Indian who forced Little Bird when crazy with firewater. Next day he ran away, knowing that Black Feather would kill him."

She continued in a slightly louder tone. "Little Bird loves Black Feather, listens to him always. Understand now, that was wrong. Storm say Little Bird must think for self."

The Indian girl put her hand over Sarah's. "Because of lie, Little Bird will not hold Storm to promise. You love Storm, Storm loves you—Little Bird happy, not sad. Little Bird have baby. Little Sarah make Little Bird very happy.

"We leave ranch, but not go far. Storm sending Little Bird to Indian school. He start bank account for Little Sarah. She go to school, too, someday. Until Little Bird's ready for school, live on reservation with grandmother. Storm promises to talk with grandmother, make her welcome Little Bird and Little Sarah."

Sarah embraced the Indian girl fondly.

"You still want this bad Indian for sister?"

"Oh, Little Bird, I'm so happy for you. I forgive everything.

156

You are very brave to admit the truth. I'm proud to be your sister." She hugged Little Bird again. "Now, let's make you pretty for the party tonight."

The little yard behind Manny and Emily's cottage was gaily decorated with candles and lamps, adding excitement to the night air. A colorful cloth covered each table, though neither showed under all the food Emily placed on them. Chairs were scattered in half circles around the yard, where Emily and Manny scurried to seat everyone comfortably.

Sarah arrived early with Dawn and Little Bird. Dawn had dressed proudly in an Indian costume of white buckskin, and with her dark beauty in the green satin, Little Bird stunned everyone, especially Snakebite, who followed her the whole evening.

To her delight, Sarah found a well-scrubbed and groomed crew awaiting her with sheepish grins. She sat and conversed with each, wondering why Storm had not made an appearance. She approached Hunter with the question, but he merely shrugged.

Just before Emily announced that the tables of food were ready, Storm appeared dressed in a clean white shirt and dark pants. Immediately he made his way to Sarah's side, planting a tender kiss on her temple. Sarah smiled up at him. Their eyes locked. Both knew nothing stood in their way any longer. Their exchanged look revealed love, relief, and a "let's talk alone, soon" plea. Words no longer necessary, their eyes did all the conversing.

They ate with the others, laughing and joking congenially, but their eyes still caressed each other and begged to be alone. As the guests finished eating and broke into small groups Storm steered Sarah to the rear of the yard, where no lights or eyes could follow them.

Sarah expected to be embraced and smothered with kisses of joy and promises, but he held her at arm's length, peering into her eyes by the light of the slightest sliver of a moon.

"Little Bird talked to you. I can tell by the joy in your eyes," he said.

"Yes, but how did you get her to admit Wilson didn't father her baby?"

"Actually, it was you who got her to admit it."

"Me? I don't understand."

"Little Bird has been breaking down little by little all along, from your love. You loved your enemy, not just into friendship, but also into the Kingdom of God. We prayed together this afternoon. You set such a fine example of Christian love, she now wants to be *just like you!*

"It was my giving up the ranch that finally broke Little Bird, but only because you had already brought her to the breaking point."

He paused, staring down at her tenderly. "Sarah, do you understand what this means?"

"That you're no longer promised to another. You're free."

He continued to stare into her eyes, as if scanning them for her true feelings. "Will you marry me, Sarah Clarke?"

"Yes," she whispered, without hesitation.

Still holding her at arm's length, he asked, "I want you to understand something. I may be half white to you, but in the eyes of the community, I'm just another Indian. They don't accept *half* Indian. You're either Indian or white. You had a taste of that attitude when Samuel Lewis visited. It could be like that for a long time."

She started to reply, "But it doesn't—"

Storm put his finger to her lips. "When I go into a town, I'm sometimes tolerated, other times I'm ridiculed. I've been shot at and had stones hurled. Name calling is common, and there are places I'm not allowed to enter.

"Also keep in mind, if we marry and have children, they will also be Indian and subjected to the same treatment."

Storm had given her much to think about—things that had never occurred to her. She stood silently, staring into his eyes, without an answer.

Suddenly he crushed her to him. "I love you, Sarah, more than I've ever loved anyone or anything." He gritted his teeth together and said emotionally, "It's because I care so much that I want you aware of what you're getting yourself into by marrying me."

Storm loosened his hold on her so he could search her eyes again. "You thought love was all that we needed, but there is so much more to consider. It would be simpler for me to marry an Indian, and you a white man."

Sarah laid her head on Storm's chest and listened to his heart beating. *God lives in this heart; God loves this heart; this heart loves me and beats for me.* How she loved Storm's heart! Each and every beat.

She looked up at him, "I won't like the attitude of the community, and I'll hate having our children treated badly. But God loves you; you belong to Him. He loves me; I belong to Him. Our children— God will love them, too, and they Him. We'll all be able to endure whatever life hands us, as long as we keep near to Him."

Sarah put her chin up proudly. "I *will* marry you, Storm. I could never marry another."

Storm kissed her lips tenderly. "Thank you, Sarah." He cast his eyes heavenward, "Thank You, Lord," he whispered.